STUDENT EDITION

Resources by Mark Batterson

Be a Circle Maker

The Circle Maker

The Circle Maker Video Curriculum

The Circle Maker Prayer Journal

The Circle Maker Student Edition

Draw the Circle

In a Pit with a Lion on a Snowy Day

Praying Circles around Your Children

Primal

Soul Print

Wild Goose Chase

Mark Batterson
Parker Batterson

All IN

You are one decision away from
a totally different life.

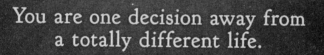 ZONDERVAN®

ZONDERVAN

All In Student Edition
Copyright © 2014 by Mark Batterson

This title is also available as a Zondervan ebook.
Visit www.zondervan.com/ebooks.

Requests for information should be addressed to:

Zondervan, *Grand Rapids, Michigan 49546*

ISBN 978-0-310-74469-6

Published in association with the literary agency of Fedd & Company, Inc., Post Office Box 34973, Austin, TX 78734.

Cover design: *Extra Credit Projects and Cindy Davis*
Interior composition: *Greg Johnson/Textbook Perfect*

Printed in the United States of America

14 15 16 17 18 19 /DCI/ 21 20 19 18 17 16 15 14 13 12 11 10 9 8 7 6 5 4 3 2 1

Dedicated to the church I have the joy
and privilege of pastoring—

National Community Church,
Washington, DC

CONTENTS

NOW OR NEVER

ALL IN

ALL OUT

ALL IN ALL

ALL OR NOTHING

NOW OR NEVER

CHAPTER 1

PACK YOUR COFFIN

A hundred years ago came a new breed of missionary: one-way missionaries. They'd buy one-way tickets to the mission field without the idea of return. Their suitcases were actual coffins where they packed what little they owned because they knew they wouldn't be returning home. They sailed out of port waving good-bye to life as they knew it.

A. W. Milne was one of those brave missionaries. He set out for the New Hebrides in the South Pacific, knowing full well that the headhunters who lived there had martyred every missionary before him. But Milne did not fear for his life, because he had already died to himself. His coffin was packed. He ended up living with the tribe for thirty-five years and loved every day of it. When he died, tribe members buried him in the middle of their village and inscribed this epitaph on his tombstone:

When he came there was no light.
When he left there was no darkness.

When did we start believing that God wants to send us to safe places to do easy things? That faithfulness is just holding the fort? That playing it safe is actually safe? That radical is anything but normal?

Come on!
Jesus didn't die to keep us safe. He died to make us dangerous.
It's time to go *all in* and *all out*.
Pack your coffin!

CHAPTER 2

THE INVERTED GOSPEL

Back in the day, there was an astronomer named Nicolaus Copernicus who challenged the belief that the earth was the center of the universe. Copernicus suggested that the sun didn't revolve around the earth, but rather that the earth revolved around the sun. The Copernican Revolution turned the scientific world upside down, and blew a lot of people's minds.

We all need to experience a little Copernican Revolution in our own lives. That change happens once we come to terms with the fact that the world doesn't revolve around *us*. That's what babies do: let the world feed them and change their diapers. But you have to grow up sometime, physically *and* spiritually. Of course, that's easier said than done.

When we're born, everything's about us. Anyone and everyone in our presence is there to serve us. It's as if we're alive solely to have people wait on us. And that's an okay mind-set if you're an infant. If you're seventeen, it's a problem!

Heads up: *You're not the center of the universe!*

All that to say, sinfulness is selfishness. It's placing yourself above all others — your desires, your "needs," your plans — above everyone else. You might still seek God, but you definitely don't seek Him first. And that's the truth. You seek Him second or third or seventh. Even if you sing "Jesus at the center of it all," what you really want to happen is for others to bow down to you because you bow down to Christ. That right there is a sneaky form of selfishness disguised as holiness, but is not truly Jesus centered. It's all about you. It's less about us serving His purposes and more about Him serving *our* purposes.

I like to call it the inverted gospel.

Who's Following Who

If you walk into most churches, most people think they're following Jesus, but I'm just not convinced. Those people might think that they are following Jesus, when actually *they've invited Jesus to follow them*. They call Him Savior, but they haven't ever given Him *everything* or really sacrificed anything significant for Him. Believe me, I used to be one of them. I wanted to go down my own path and have Jesus tag along. I wanted Jesus to follow me, to provide me with what I wanted, and to follow through with my will.

My Copernican Revolution didn't come to me until I was a nineteen-year-old freshman at the University of Chicago. This question sparked the revolution: *Lord, what do You want me to do with my life?* This question is a dangerous one to ask God, but not asking it would be ten times more dangerous.

My life became too hectic to control myself. Honestly, I didn't play God very well. Not to mention how tiring it became. I quit trying to "find myself" and decided to seek the Lord first. And I couldn't get enough of His Word! I got up early to pray. I *actually* fasted for the first time in my life — I really meant business. I had never truly put God first, but this time I did.

On my last day of summer vacation, I woke up at the crack

of dawn to walk around and pray. My family and I had taken a vacation at Lake Ida in Alexandria, Minnesota. The cow pasture I walked through may as well have been the backside of the Sinai Desert with a burning bush. God's presence was *obvious*. Months after first asking God, I finally got an answer from Him. At that moment, I knew what God wanted me to do with my life.

The first day of my sophomore year, I took the first step toward God's plan for me. I walked into the admissions office at the University of Chicago to tell them that I was transferring to a Bible college in Springfield, Missouri to pursue ministry full time. It's safe to say that the guidance counselor thought I was out of my mind. Most of my friends and family thought I was making a mistake too. I was giving up a *full-ride scholarship* to one of the top-ranked universities in the country. Sometimes it didn't even make sense to *me*. It was obvious that the most logical thing in the situation would have been to finish my undergrad studies at U of C and then go to seminary *after*. But that wasn't what I was going to do. I knew what God was telling me to do, and this was my now-or-never moment to show God that I truly did mean business. I knew I needed to quit going with the course of everyday life, push all my chips to the middle of the table, and go all in with God.

Did this decision completely alter my life? Immediately. Did I ever second guess myself? More than once! But I knew that my amazing adventure with Jesus would never begin until I took that step. That day I finally stopped asking Jesus to follow me, and I started following Him.

Let me ask the question: *Who's following who*?

Are you following Jesus?

Or have you made it your game and asked Jesus to follow you?

Holy Dare

More than a hundred years ago, a bold Brit made a crazy statement that would challenge generations to come: "The world has yet to see what God will do with and for and through and in and by the man who is fully and wholly consecrated to Him."[1]

D. L. Moody heard that call first. They weren't empty words that were *just* words. They messed with his mind and seeped into his soul. That call to complete dedication would define his life. And his life, in turn, defined dedication.

It was Moody's *all in* moment.

Maybe this is yours?

In *The Circle Maker Student Edition*, the prequel to this book, you may have read about the importance of prayer. Prayer turns *your* best efforts into God's best efforts. You've got to pray a circle around the promises of God the same way the Israelites circled Jericho. And you keep circling until He answers. But you can't just pray like it depends on God. You also have to *work* like it depends on you. You can't just draw the circle. You have to draw a line in the sand.

You are only one decision away from a totally different life. And it may be the toughest decision you'll ever make. But if you have the courage to completely surrender yourself to the freedom Jesus offers, there is no telling what God will do. All bets are off because all bets are on God.

D. L. Moody left a permanent imprint on his generation. Even now, his passion for the gospel continues to influence millions of people through Moody Church, Moody Bible Institute, and Moody Publishers. That's epic.

Moody left an amazing legacy, but it all started with his dedication. It always does. And nothing has changed. The world has yet to see what God will do with and for and through and in and by the man who is fully and wholly consecrated to Him. It's still true.

Why not you?
Why not now?

Amazing Things

Before God does the crazy miracles we often hear about in other people's lives, they usually consecrate themselves to God, which means they decide to be 100 percent committed and devoted and dedicated to God.

> *"Consecrate yourselves, for tomorrow the LORD will do amazing things among you."*

Here's our ultimate problem: *we try to do God's job for Him.* We want to do amazing things for God. And that seems cool and noble and all, but we've got it backward. God wants to do amazing things *for* us. That's His job, not ours. Our job is consecration. That's it. And if we do our job, God will definitely do His.

Here's a taste of what consecration is NOT:

- Going to church once a week like good little boys and girls.
- Daily devotions, done by waking up 4.7 minutes earlier than normal.
- Fasting during Lent. Not even eating chocolate.
- Keeping the Ten Commandments.
- Sharing your faith with friends who need "saving."
- Giving God the tithe.
- Repeating the sinner's prayer. Not even twenty times.
- It's not volunteering for a ministry.
- It's not leading a small group.
- It's not raising your hands when you're singing.
- It's not going on a mission trip.

All of those things are fine things, but that isn't necessarily consecration. It's more than behavior modification. It's more than conformity to some moral code. It's more than just doing good deeds to cancel out the bad. It's something deeper, and much truer.

I want to break that zing you feel when you hear "consecration." It sounds so Christianese, and I bet you've heard a thousand and one sermons about not sinning. The actual word *consecrate* means to *set yourself apart*. By definition, consecration demands *full devotion*. It's taking your butt off Jesus' throne. There's so much to it. It's giving up pure self-interest. It's giving God veto power. It's surrendering *all of you* to *all of Him*. It's recognizing that every second of time, every last ounce of energy, and every penny of money is a gift *from* God and *for* God. Consecration is an ever-deepening love for Jesus, a childlike trust in the heavenly Father, and a blind obedience to the Holy Spirit. Consecration is a lot more, but let's keep it simple. Here's my personal definition of consecration:

Consecration is going *all in* and *all out* for the *All in All*.

All In

My greatest concern as a pastor is that people can go to church every week of their lives and never go *all in* with Jesus Christ. They'll follow the rules but never follow Christ. We've cheapened the gospel by allowing people to buy in without selling out (even though Jesus says to sell *everything*.) We've made it way too convenient, and too comfortable. We've given people just enough Jesus to be bored but not enough to feel the surge of holy adrenaline that courses through your veins when you decide to follow Him no matter what, no matter where, no matter when.

A guy from Denmark named Søren Kierkegaard believed that boredom was the root of all evil. In other words, boredom isn't just boring. It's wrong. You cannot be in the presence of God and be bored at the same time. You just can't be in the will of God and be bored at the same time. If you follow in the footsteps of Jesus, it will be anything but boring.

The choice is yours — consecration or boredom? If you don't consecrate and dedicate yourself to Christ, you'll get bored. If you do, you won't. And that is where the battle is won or lost. If you don't go all in, you'll never get into the Promised Land. But if you go all out, God will part the Jordan River so you can cross through on dry ground.

Stop trying to do God's job for Him. You don't have to do amazing things. You can't do amazing things. *Amazing always begins with consecration*. And just like amazing always begins with consecration, *consecration always ends with amazing*. I'm telling you! Something crazy good always happens on *day two* of my fasts.

When you look back on your life, the greatest moments will be the ones where you went all in. It's as true today as it was the day Abraham placed Isaac on the altar, the day Jonathan climbed a cliff to fight the Philistines, and the day Peter got out of the boat and walked on water.

In the pages that follow, you're about to read about some amazing all in moments. They're defining moments in Scripture. I'll also share stories of ordinary people who're making an extraordinary difference with their lives. Hopefully, they'll inspire you to risk more, sacrifice more, and dream more.

The longer I follow Jesus, the more convinced I am of this simple truth: God doesn't do what God does *because of* us. God does what God does *in spite of* us. All you have to do is stay out of the way.

Stay humble. Stay hungry.

If you aren't hungry for God, you are full of yourself. That's why God cannot fill you with His Spirit. But if you'll empty yourself, if you'll die to self, you'll be a different person by the time you reach the last page of this book. As I wrote this book, I prayed that God would rewrite your life. I also prayed that God would rewrite history through your life!

CHAPTER 3

DRAW
THE
LINE

"Take up your cross daily, and follow me."

Luke 9:23 NLT

In AD 44, King Herod ordered that James the Greater be thrust through with a sword. He was the first of the apostles to be martyred. And so the bloodbath began. Luke was hung by the neck from an olive tree in Greece. Doubting Thomas was stabbed with a pine spear, tortured with red-hot plates, and burned alive in India. In AD 54, the proconsul of Hierapolis had Philip tortured and crucified because his wife converted to Christianity while listening to Philip preach. Philip continued to preach while on the cross. Matthew was stabbed in the back in Ethiopia. Bartholomew was flogged to death in Armenia. James the Just was thrown off the top of the temple in Jerusalem. After surviving the one-hundred-foot fall, he was clubbed to death by a mob. Simon the Zealot was crucified by the governor of Syria in AD 74. Judas Thaddeus was beaten to death with sticks in Mesopotamia. Matthias, who replaced Judas Iscariot, was stoned to death and then beheaded. And Peter was crucified upside down at his own request. John the Beloved is the only disciple to die of natural causes, but that's only because he survived his own execution. When a cauldron of boiling oil couldn't kill John, Emperor Diocletian exiled him to the island of Patmos, where he lived until his death in AD 95.

Every Christian living in a first-world country in the twenty-first century should read *Foxe's Book of Martyrs*. It's a reality check that puts our first-world problems into perspective. This sets the standard for sacrifice. Our risks seem rather tame and most of our sacrifices seem pretty lame by comparison.

Our normal is so subnormal that normal seems radical. To the first-century disciples, normal and radical were synonyms. We've turned them into antonyms.

In Luke 9:23 – 24, Jesus threw down the gauntlet with his disciples. He wanted to see who was in and who was out. Or more accurately, who was *all in.*

> *"Whoever wants to be my disciple must deny themselves and take up their cross daily and follow me. For whoever wants to save their life will lose it, but whoever loses their life for me will save it."*

The disciples took that literally. We can at least take it figuratively. I'm not suggesting we *will* die physically for Christ, but we *must* die to ourselves. If Jesus hung on His cross, we can certainly carry ours! It's our highest privilege and greatest responsibility.

Anything less than the complete surrender of our lives to the lordship of Jesus Christ is robbing God of the glory He demands and deserves. It's also cheating ourselves out of the eternal reward God has reserved for us.

We won't come alive, in the truest and fullest sense, until we die to self. And we won't find ourselves until we lose ourselves in the cause of Christ.

It's time to ante up.

It's time to go all in.

If Jesus is not Lord *of all*, then Jesus is not Lord *at all*.
It's all or nothing.
It's now or never.

The Americanized Gospel

We have Americanized the gospel and spiritualized the American Dream. Am I right or am I right? But neither one comes close to the true gospel. When you try to add something to the gospel, you're not enhancing it. You're ruining it! The gospel, in its purest form, is as good as it gets.

We want God on our terms, but that's just not how we "get" God. That's how we get false, obnoxious religion. You only get a relationship with God on His terms. It's not like we have any abilities (like making time stand still) that God *needs*. God is perfect and loving, so just take what He offers!

The apostle Paul defines the deal that is on the table this way:

God made him who had no sin to be sin for us, so that in him we might become the righteousness of God.

The moment you bow your knee to the lordship of Jesus, all of your sin is transferred to Christ's account and erased from yours. He already paid for it. It was nailed to the cross two thousand years ago! But that's only half the gospel. Mercy is *not* getting what you deserve — the wrath of God. Grace is getting what you *don't* deserve — the righteousness of Christ. Everything you've done wrong is forgiven and forgotten! And then God calls it even.

It's like God says, "I'll take the blame and shame for everything you did wrong and give you credit for everything I did right." It doesn't get any better than that, and that's why it's called the gospel. It's good news ... the best news!

The gospel costs nothing. We can't buy it, and especially can't earn it. It can only be received as a free gift, through God's grace.

It costs nothing, but it demands everything. And that's where most of us get stuck. We're too Christian to enjoy sin and too sinful to enjoy Christ. We've got just enough Jesus to be informed, but not enough to be *transformed*. And transformation is where it's at.

We want everything God has to offer without giving anything up. We want to keep sinning, but get the cool miracles and God's favor on the side. And then we get mad at God when He doesn't deliver. What!? We're afraid that if we commit to God, we'll miss out on what this life has to offer. Lie! It's the same lie the serpent told Adam and Eve in the garden. God's not holding out on you.

You can take Psalm 84:11 to the bank:

No good thing does God withhold from those who walk uprightly.

If you don't hold out on God, I can promise you this: God will not hold out on you. But it's all or nothing.

It's *all of you* for *all of Him*.

No Sacrifice

Let me put my cards on the table.

I don't think anyone has ever sacrificed anything for God. If you've only "sacrificed" what God's already given you, have you sacrificed anything at all? At the end of the day, Judgment Day, our only regret will be whatever we didn't give back to God.

The key to self-fulfillment is self-denial, and by self-denial, I mean delayed gratification. And by delay, I don't mean days or months or years. I mean a lifetime. Our delayed gratification on earth will carry over to heaven. We'll talk more about delayed gratification in a few chapters.

The selfish part of us has a little freak-out allergic reaction to the word *deny*. It's tough to do when we live in the lap of luxury. Listen: the biggest problem with indulgence (the luxury we experience is America) is that *enough is never enough*. The more we indulge ourselves in food or sex or any of the other toys we have, the less we'll enjoy them. It's not until we go *all in* with God that we discover that true joy is only found on the sacrificial side of life.

The more you give away, the more you will enjoy what you have. True story. If you give God the tithe, you'll enjoy the 90 percent you keep 10 percent more. Which also means you'll enjoy the 80 percent you keep 20 percent more! And eventually you'll enjoy the 70 percent you keep 30 percent more! And so on. One of our life goals as a family is to reverse tithe and live off 10 percent and give away 90 percent. When we get there, I'm confident we'll enjoy the 10 percent we keep 90 percent more.

You probably heard this classy playground rule when you were a kid: *finders keepers, losers weepers*. It's the exact opposite in God's kingdom: *finders weepers, losers keepers*. The first will be last and the last will be first.

The Rich Young Ruler

On paper, the Rich Young Ruler is the *bomb*. He's the epitome of religiosity! But religion and hypocrisy are kissing cousins. In reality, the Rich Young Ruler is the opposite of what it means to be all in. His life is a standing warning: *if we hold out on God, we'll miss out on everything God wants to do in us and for us* and *through us*. Of course, the good news is that the flip side is true as well.

I haven't met many people possessed by demons, but I've met a lot of people possessed by their possessions! They don't own things. Things own them. Have you ever met someone like that? People who cry when they get a scratch on their car, or throw a fit if they crack their phone screen? That's true of the Rich Young Ruler. He had everything money could buy. He had his whole life in front of him. He called his own shots. But something was obviously missing. The emptiness in his soul is evident when he asks Jesus:

What am I still missing?

This player had everything we think we want. He's rich, young, and powerful. What more could he possibly want? Why was he so miserable? The answer's easy: he was *following the rules*, but he wasn't *following Jesus*. And I think that is true of far too many people in far too many churches.

The text says he kept *all* the commandments. He didn't do a thing wrong, but you can do nothing wrong and still do nothing right. By definition, righteousness is doing something right. We've reduced it to doing nothing wrong. And spending your whole life trying to do nothing wrong will leave you asking the same question the Rich Young Ruler did: *What am I still missing?* That's why people try religion and then quit!

We fixate on sins of commission: *Don't do this and don't do that — and you're okay!* But that's holiness by subtraction. And it's more hypocrisy than holiness! It's the sins of omission — what you would've, could've, and should've done — that break God's heart.

The heavenly Father is preparing good works in advance with our name written in Helvetica bold on them. He's ordering our footsteps. And He's able to do immeasurably more than all we can ask or imagine. As in, you can't measure what He can and wants to do with you. But we can't just play defense. We have to play offense! We can't just do nothing wrong. We have to do something right. We can't just follow the rules. We have to follow *Jesus*.

The story of the Rich Young Ruler is one of the saddest stories in the Bible because he had so much potential. He could have used his resources, his network, and his energy to do some insane good, but he spent it all on himself. He thought that was what would make him happy, but that was what made him miserable.

The Rich Young Ruler eventually became the Old Rich Ruler. I don't know what he was thinking on his deathbed, but I have a hunch. It was the moment Jesus said, "Follow me." Those words echoed in his ear until the day he died. It was the opportunity of a lifetime, but he didn't have the guts to go for it.

Check out the parable of the bags of gold. The man who got one bag buried it in the ground. He ultimately gave back to the master exactly what the master had given him. And to be perfectly honest, that's not half bad in a recession. He broke even. But Jesus called him *wicked*.

That seems like a little bit of an overreaction doesn't it? In fact, I'd be tempted to pull a Peter and take Jesus aside and tell Him to dial it back just a bit. But when I think Jesus is wrong, it's always something wrong with me. I'm missing the point somewhere. The man who buried his bag of gold wasn't willing to gamble on God. He didn't even ante up! And that's the point of this parable: faith is pushing all of your chips to the middle of the table.

> *"If you want to be perfect, go, sell your possessions and give to the poor, and you will have treasure in heaven. Then come, follow me."*

Accumulate Experiences

Be honest: Have you ever felt bad for the Rich Young Ruler? Part of me feels like Jesus was asking for too much. *Are You sure You want to ask for everything? Why don't You start with the tithe?* But Jesus goes right in with the sucker punch. He asks the poor guy to cough it *all* up! Why? Because He loved the Rich Young Ruler too much to ask for anything less!

We focus on what Jesus asked him to *give up* but fail to consider what He *offered* in exchange. Jesus invited the Rich Young Ruler to *follow* Him. That's the offer of a lifetime, right there!

I live in the internship capital of the world. Trillions of twenty-somethings flock to D.C. every summer because the right internship with the right person can open the right door. It's all about building your résumé. I don't think anyone in the history of humankind has ever been offered a better internship opportunity than the Rich Young Ruler. An internship with the Creator of the Universe? Come on, that'll look good on a job application. What a reference! But the Rich Young Ruler says *no*. What!?

So if you feel bad for the Rich Young Ruler, it shouldn't be because of what Jesus asked him to give up. It should be because of the opportunity he passed up.

The average person never traveled outside a thirty-mile radius of their home in Jesus' time, but He sent His disciples to the ends of the earth. These uneducated fishermen, who would've lived their entire lives within a stone's throw of the Sea of Galilee, traveled all over the ancient world and turned it upside down. These guys are the original migrating hippies.

Think about their experiences during their three-year internship with Jesus. They went camping, hiking, fishing, and sailing with the *Son of God*. Every parable Jesus told, they were in the front row, and then they hung out with Him backstage. They didn't just witness His miracles. They filleted the miraculous catch of fish, fried it, and ate it. They literally ate Jesus' miracle

The disciples were poor as dirt in terms of material possessions, but they had such an amazing a wealth of experiences. The Rich Young Ruler gave that up because he couldn't let go of his possessions. That's sad. Matthew was a tax collector and he did it, so it's not like it's impossible. But Richie Rich couldn't quite do it.

Don't accumulate possessions. Accumulate experiences!

Senior Partner

I have a ninety-five-year-old friend named Stanley Tam. More than a half century ago, Stanley made a defining decision to go all in with God. Stanley legally transferred 51 percent of the shares of his company to God. It took three lawyers to pull it off, because the first two thought he was bonkers!

Stanley started the United States Plastic Corporation with $37. When he gave his business back to God, annual revenues were like $200,000. But Stanley believed God would bless his business, and he wanted to honor God from the beginning.

At that point, most of us would have been patting ourselves on the back. Not Stanley. He felt *bad* for keeping 49 percent for himself. After reading the parable about the merchant who sold everything to obtain the pearl of great price, Stanley dumped all his shares.

I love Stanley's plainspoken words: "A man can eat only one meal at a time, wear only one suit of clothes at a time, drive only one car at a time. All this I have. Isn't that enough?"

On January 15, 1955, every share of stock was transferred to his Senior Partner (that'd be God), and Stanley became a salaried employee of the company he had started. That is the day Stanley went *all in* with God. From that day to the present, Stanley has given away more than $120 million.

I love telling Stanley's story because he's my hero. This guy is legit. It also makes me look in the mirror at myself. I can tell you I'm all in, but you need to look at how I spend my *time* and my *money*. Those two things reveal my true priorities. So let me ask you: is God your Senior Partner?

Draw the Line

Destiny is not a mystery. Destiny is a decision. And you're only one decision away from a totally different life. One decision can totally turn you around. One decision can radically alter a relationship. One decision can lead toward health — spiritual, physical, or emotional. And those defining decisions will become the defining moments of your life.

For Stanley Tam, the defining moment was January 15, 1955.

What risk do you need to take?

What sacrifice do you need to make?

This isn't a book to read. It's a decision to be made. If you read this book without making a defining decision, I wasted my time writing it and you wasted your time reading it. At some point, on some page, you'll feel the Holy Spirit prompting you to act decisively. Don't ignore it. Obey it. No seriously. If you need to stop reading right now, turn to the back and write a defining decision you need to make on the back inside cover.

We'll talk more about them in upcoming chapters, but there are some heroes who have gone all in. And we should follow suit.

You need to put Isaac on the altar like Abraham.

You need to throw down your staff like Moses.

You need to burn your plowing equipment like Elisha.

You need to climb the cliff like Jonathan.

You need to get out of the boat like Peter.

There comes a moment when you need to go *all in*.

This is that moment.

This is your moment.

CHAPTER 4

CHARGE

Joshua Chamberlain knew nothing about being a soldier. He was a student of theology and a professor of rhetoric. But when duty called, Chamberlain answered. Then he climbed the ranks to become Colonel of the 20th Maine Volunteer Infantry Regiment, Union Army.

On July 2, 1863, three hundred soldiers were all that stood between the Confederates and certain defeat at a battlefield in Gettysburg, Pennsylvania. Ring a bell? Abraham Lincoln gave a famous speech there, but he wouldn't have had the opportunity without the courage of one Colonel Chamberlain.

At 2:30 PM, the first of the attacks came. The 15th and 47th Alabama Infantry Regiments of the Confederate Army charged toward Chamberlain, but they held their ground. There were five charges following, but they still didn't budge, despite the fact that only eighty men were left standing. Chamberlain was even hit by a bullet in the belt buckle. It knocked him down, but the 34 year-old schoolteacher got right back up.

This was his date with destiny.

When a sergeant informed Chamberlain that there were no reinforcements on the way and his men had one round of ammunition left, he knew he needed to act decisively. The sensible thing to do would have been to wave the white flag and surrender, but that thought didn't cross Chamberlain's mind. The decision he made was a game changer for the entire war, and single-handedly saved the Union. He caught the enemy totally off-guard by climbing onto the barricade and ordered his men to: "Charge!"

Despite being outnumbered fifty-to-one, his men fixed their bayonets and charged down the Little Round Top. By successfully executing a great right wheel, Chamberlain won one of the most improbable victories in military history. Four thousand confederates surrendered to eighty Union soldiers!

That one act of courage saved the Union. Historians believe that if Chamberlain had not chosen to charge, the confederates would have gained the upper hand. If the rebels had won that one battle, they probably would have won the Civil War altogether, and history would have been radically altered. The courage of one man saved the day, saved the army, saved the Union.

It reminds me of the old Proverb:

> For want of a shoe the horse was lost.
> For want of a horse the rider was lost.
> For want of a rider the message was lost.
> For want of a message the battle was lost.
> For want of a battle the kingdom was lost.
> All for the want of a horseshoe nail.

In the eyes of God, little things are big things! And I've learned that if we act on the little things, as if they are big things, then God will perform big things as if they are the little things. And that is how God's kingdom advances. Going all in is the courage to do something without looking back, or questioning your moves. Just like Elisha, we need to burn the plows so there isn't even an option of returning to previous ways.

The Inability to Do Nothing

After the war, Joshua Chamberlain didn't fall off the radar. He was voted to serve the state of Maine as its thirty-second governor. He also served as the president of his alma mater, Bowdoin College. Thirty years after his act of heroism, in 1893, he was awarded the Medal of Honor by President Grover Cleveland for "holding his position on the Little Round Top against repeated assaults, and carrying the advance position on the Great Round Top."

As Chamberlain got older, he would reflect back on his thoughts on that very day with these words: "I had deep within me the inability to do nothing. I knew I may die, but I also knew that I would not die with a bullet in my back."

The inability to do nothing!

Jesus set this very standard for us!

Without any troops, Jesus charged the money changers in the temple by turning their tables upside down and driving out their flocks. It was His Little Round Top. He confronted the Pharisees' hypocrisy. He exorcised a demon from a possessed man whom anyone else would be afraid to confront. And he stopped a funeral procession and raised a boy from the dead.

I would not call Jesus someone who was passive. He was the definition of passion. In fact, the last week of His life is referred to as "Passion Week." So despite the different personality types of His followers, we should possess the same kind of passion. Going all in means defying the "rules" of religion that the world has created to genuinely go after God — just like the prostitute who crashed a party at a Pharisee's home to anoint Jesus.

When will we realize that indecision is a decision?

When will we come to terms with the fact that inaction is an action?

God never meant for the church to be a noun. When we turn it into a noun, it becomes a turnoff. The church becomes nothing more than a club, a clique. God intended for the church to be a verb — an action verb.

Two thousand years ago, Jesus gave us the command to charge.

And He's never looked back.

Play Offense

There's an old saying: opportunity knocks. It's a lie! Usually, you are the one who needs to do the knocking. And sometimes you even have to knock the door down!

Don't wait for it to come to you. You need to go get it.

Don't just sit around, waiting for something to happen. Make it happen!

I love the story about how my friend, Bob Goff, got into law school. He's now a successful lawyer with his own firm and he's even an adjunct law professor at Pepperdine University. Success did not come easy. Bob was actually rejected from admission when he first applied. For an entire week, Bob decided to sit outside of the dean's office, every single day, all day. Bob knew the dean could admit him, and that was his answer to why he was sitting there once the dean asked. Bob would not budge until he got what he came for. And finally, the dean told him to go out and buy books because anybody with that much devotion deserves a shot.

That is going all in: *not taking no for an answer.*

What we need is a sanctified stubborn streak!

For what it's worth, Joshua Chamberlain said the only reason he couldn't give up, even when things looked completely hopeless, was the fact that he was truly a stubborn man. Referring to himself in the third person, Chamberlain said, "Their leader had no real knowledge of warfare or tactics. I was only a stubborn man and that was my greatest advantage in this fight."

The unwillingness to give up is part of going all in.

It doesn't matter how many times you've been knocked down, only how many you've gotten up.

It doesn't matter how tough it has been before, but only that you continue the fight.

As we'll see, Abraham wanted a son more than anything. He

had been looking forward to having one for what seemed like forever. And when God finally came through on the twenty-five year promise, Abraham passed the ultimate test by putting Isaac back on the altar.

Is there a dream you've given up on?

Go back and try again. Don't give up!

Failure isn't the opposite of success. It's the nearest ally!

I could have given up after a failed church plant, but I got back up and tried again. I could have given up after thirteen years of attempting to write a book, but I didn't wave the white flag.

Everyone has had a moment in their life when their dreams seemed so far off that they couldn't think of anything else to do but give up. You might even be heavily tempted right now to give up on your plans for college or your dream job. Hang in there. Even if there's no back-up and no ammunition, you need to charge the problem, charge the dream, charge the goal.

Stop talking yourself out of it! Seize the opportunity.

Stop playing defense and start playing offense.

You need to charge your goals.

You need to charge kingdom causes.

You need to charge Jesus.

CHAPTER 5

THIS IS ONLY A TEST

Some time later God tested Abraham. He said to him, "Abraham!"

"Here I am," he replied.

Then God said, "Take your son, your only son, whom you love—Isaac—and go to the region of Moriah. Sacrifice him there as a burnt offering on a mountain I will show you."

Genesis 22:1–2

That's tough to swallow. How could a loving heavenly Father even suggest something like this? But honestly, it's the biblical stories that cause the most discomfort to our logical minds that usually have the best revelations. We like to read stories like this one as if God's on trial, but it's not *His* character that is in question, it's *ours*. And that's precisely why God tests us.

You've probably seen this little pop-up on TV at some point:

This is a test. For the next sixty seconds, this station will conduct a test of the Emergency Broadcast System. This is only a test.

God never planned on letting Abraham *actually* sacrifice his son. It was only a test. He wanted see if Abe was willing to obey the most absurd command imaginable. The story reads, "God tested Abraham." And Abraham passed with flying colors. That's how you get a testimony; you *have to pass the test*.

No test = No testimony.

I didn't get a testimony in seminary or church. You don't get a testimony by listening to a lecture or sermon or speech in the comfortable confines of a classroom, church, or conference. You get a testimony in the wilderness like Moses, on the Sea of Galilee like Peter, or on the mountain like Abraham.

The Proving Ground

According to Jewish tradition, God gave Abraham ten different tests. This one is the final exam. It was specifically designed to test whether or not Abraham was all in. And this bad boy was pass or fail.

God tests us for two primary reasons.

First, it's an opportunity for God to prove Himself to us.

Second, it's an opportunity for us to prove ourselves to God.

Tests are the proving grounds. Honestly I know some people who've been "saved" for twenty-five years, but they really only have one year of experience repeated twenty-five times. It's like those kids you go to retreat or camp or conferences and want to accept Jesus into their heart *every single time*! They live at square one. That's not how you grow! They aren't learning what God's trying to teach them.

When Abraham raised the knife, God knew that Abraham was all in because he was willing to sacrifice what was most precious to him. And God proved Himself as Provider. If Abraham hadn't gone all in, he would have robbed God of the opportunity to provide. After all, God can't reveal His faithfulness until we exercise our faith. But because Abraham went all in, God revealed Himself as Jehovah-Jireh, *God our Provider*.

According to one Jewish rabbi, the ram God provided on Mount Moriah was created at twilight on the sixth day of creation for the specific purpose of taking Isaac's place on the altar. The ram grazed under the tree of life in the Garden of Eden until the very moment Abraham needed it. That's not in the Bible, so who knows if it's true, but that's an amazing thought isn't it! Long before God laid the foundation of the earth, He provided everything we'd ever need. Give Him an opportunity to prove Himself faithful. I dare you.

ID Your Isaac

God will never tempt you. He can't. On the contrary, He promises to provide an escape route for every tempting situation. But I can promise you this: God *will* test your faith. And those tests won't get easier. They'll probably get harder. Sorry! And those tests always involve what's most important to you.

What do you find your identity in?

That's your Isaac.

God will test you to make sure your identity is in Jesus Christ and nothing else.

You don't have to live in fear that God is going to take away what's most important to you. After all, Isaac was God's gift to Abraham. But if the gift ever becomes more important than the Gift Giver, then there's a problem. When you love something more than the Lord, it's the beginning of the end spiritually because you've successfully inverted the gospel.

God-given gifts are great things and dangerous things. One of my constant prayers is this: *Lord, don't let my gifts take me farther than my character can sustain me.* As we grow in the gifts God has given us, it's easy to start relying on those gifts instead of relying on God. That's when our greatest strength becomes our greatest weakness.

It was God who gave Lucifer a beautiful voice. Those musical gifts were originally used to glorify God! Then Lucifer started looking in the mirror (which is always dangerous!). He glorified the gift he had been given instead of glorifying God. Don't be a Lucifer. And remember this: *whatever you don't turn into praise turns into pride.*

What are your greatest gifts?

That's your Isaac.

The Death of a Dream

A little while ago, I met Phil Vischer, the creator of VeggieTales. It was sort of surreal hearing the voice of Bob the Tomato on a real-life person. Phil started out with loose change and a God-idea called Big Idea, Inc. The company sold more than fifty million videos and grossed hundreds of millions of dollars, but it all ended with one lawsuit. As Phil himself said, "Fourteen years' worth of work flashed before my eyes — the characters, the songs, the impact, the letters from kids all over the world. It all flashed before my eyes, then it all vanished."

Big Idea declared bankruptcy, and the dream died a painful death. That's when Phil heard some good words that saved his soul.

> *If God gives you a dream, and the dream comes to life and God shows up in it, and then the dream dies, it may be that God wants to see what is more important to you — the dream or him.*

Which do you love more: the dream or the God who gave you the dream?

Every dream I've ever had has gone through a death and a resurrection. Look at my writing dream! I feel as called to write as I do to pastor, but a half dozen manuscripts were buried alive on my hard drive before my first book, *In a Pit with a Lion on a Snowy Day*, was published. And that book had to go through a death and resurrection as well. The editors had me shred the first manuscript and write the entire book a second time.

Dreams aren't just born. They're reborn. You have to put them on the altar and raise the knife. And once the dream is dead and buried, it can be resurrected for God's glory.

The Dream Maker

The Holy Spirit is the Dream Maker. He's the one who sparks the synapses in your right-brain imagination. If you're walking next to the Holy Spirit, He'll give you some excellent God-ideas. He'll become the arrows on your compass.

I recently met John Kilcullen at a writer's conference. John's writing journey began with a passing comment that became a lifelong passion: "Do you have any simple books on Microsoft DOS — something like DOS for dummies?" That tiny question became a pretty famous brand of books, *For Dummies*. With more than sixteen hundred titles in thirty-one languages, *For Dummies* books have sold more than sixty million copies!

I'd rather have one God-idea than a thousand good ideas. Good ideas are good, but God-ideas change the course of history. You can get good ideas in a lot of different places — classrooms, conferences, and bookstores. But God-ideas only come from one place — the Holy Spirit Himself. I'm telling you, if you listen closely, you'll hear some crazy things.

Isaac was God's idea. It was God who promised Abraham a son and gave the promise through Sarah. Postmenopausal octogenarians don't get pregnant. Period. But God always delivers!

My Isaac

I genuinely think that the church ought to be the most creative place on the planet. There are ways of "doing church" that no one's thought of yet. That driving motivation is what gets me up early and keeps me up late. And my passion to do church differently was put there by the Holy Spirit! I have no doubt that God is the one who called me (and gave me the gifts) to serve as lead pastor of NCC, but it also means NCC is my Isaac.

I can honestly say I wouldn't want be doing anything else. I hope you get a job as great as this! I've invested sixteen years of blood, sweat, and tears into this dream called National Community Church, and I pray that I serve there for the rest of my life on earth. I absolutely love what I do. But if I love it more than I love God, then the very thing God has called me to do is no longer serving His purposes. It's serving *my* purposes and keeping *me* happy and comfy.

I never use the possessive pronoun *my* when I refer to the church. I love when NCCers refer to it as *their* church, because it is! But I'm careful not to. Christ is the Shepherd. As pastor, I'm the under-shepherd. I always want to remember it's not *my* church. It's *His* church.

The truth of the matter is that you can't really say *mine* about anything! Nothing belongs to you — not your house, not your car, not your clothes, and not your life. Every material thing you own (including your body) is the by-product of the time, talent, and treasure God has given you.

When you kneel at the foot of the cross, the possessive pronoun is eliminated from your vocabulary. When you're all in, there's no more *me*, *my*, or *mine*.

The early Methodists devoted themselves entirely to God with a covenant prayer. Check this out:

I am no longer my own, but Thine. Put me to what Thou wilt, rank me with whom Thou wilt; put me to doing, put me to suffering; let me be employed for Thee or laid aside for Thee, exalted for Thee or brought low for thee; let me be full, let me be empty;

let me have all things, let me have nothing; I freely and heartily yield all things to Thy pleasure and disposal.

And now, O glorious and blessed God, Father, Son, and Holy Spirit, Thou art mine, and I am Thine. So be it. And the covenant, which I have made on earth, let it be ratified in heaven. Amen.

Whose You Are

Do you find your identity in *who you are* or *whose you are*?

That subtle difference makes all the difference in the world.

You can base your identity on a thousand things — the degrees you'll get, the positions you'll hold, the salary you'll make, the trophies you've won, the hobbies you have, the way you look, the way you dress, the school you go to, the friends you have or the house you live in. But if you base your identity on any of those things, your identity is a literally a house of cards. That sucker's going to collapse sooner or later. There's one solid foundation and that's Jesus Christ. If you find security in *what you've done in the past*, you'll always fall short and you'll miss what God's doing *now*! The solution? The gospel. Boom. There's only one place in which to find your true identity and eternal security: *what Christ has done for you.*

Religion is spelled *do.*

The gospel is spelled *done.*

Going all in means 100 percent reliance on the atoning work of Christ. Done. It's not 99 percent grace and 1 percent good works. The problem is that most of us still want 1 percent credit for the things we've done right, but it's *all* grace or *no* grace. There's no partial grace. You either let God forgive you or you spend the rest of your life trying to forgive yourself. You're not a part of the equation of salvation. Sorry. You cannot trust Jesus Christ 99 percent. Trust is a 100 percent proposition.

It's addition by subtraction.

So the question is this: What do you need to give up? What do you need to put on the altar? What is getting between you and God? What feeds your ego? Where do you find your security outside of Christ?

Put That Sucker on the Altar!

The longer and harder you work on something, the harder it is to give it up. And the longer you have to wait for it, the tougher it is to give it back. That's why Abraham's all in moment is so amazing. He was waiting for Isaac for twenty-five years! And he hands it right back over to God. That's awesome. Respect.

The more God blesses you, the harder it is to keep that blessing from becoming an idol in your life. Money may be the best example. Mo' money, mo' problems. Isn't it ironic that "In God We Trust" is printed on the thing we trust God the least with? If you're financially blessed, it's a gift from God. But He blesses us more so we can be more of a blessing!

Are you willing to give everything away?

Our tendency is to loophole *everything*. *Shouldn't I save my money? Isn't that better stewardship? Doesn't the Bible tell me to leave an inheritance?* I'm not saying don't do those things. But that doesn't keep me from asking the point-blank question: Are you willing to give it all away? If you aren't, then your idol may be a piggy bank or a college savings plan.

CHAPTER 6

BURN THE SHIPS

So Elisha left him and went back. He took his yoke of oxen and slaughtered them. He burned the plowing equipment to cook the meat and gave it to the people, and they ate. Then he set out to follow Elijah and became his servant.

1 Kings 19:21

Hernán Cortés set sail for Mexico with 11 ships, 13 horses, 110 sailors, and 553 soldiers on a crisp February morning in 1519. There were close to five million natives when he arrived. The odds were stacked against him about 7,541 to 1. Two previous expeditions had failed to even establish a settlement in the New World, but, as you know from world history, Cortés conquered much of South America on his own.

What Cortés did after landing is an epic tale of mythic proportions. He issued an order that turned his mission into an all-or-nothing proposition: *Burn the ships!* Okay, who does that? And crazier, who *listens?* Anyway, as his crew watched their fleet of ships burn and sink, they realized retreat was not an option. Nine times out of ten, failure is resorting to Plan B when Plan A gets too risky or difficult. That's why most people are living their Plan B, C, D, or some people are out of plans! They don't burn the ships; heck, they don't commit to anything. Plan A people don't have a Plan B. It's Plan A or bust. They'd rather crash and burn going after their dreams than succeed at something less noble.

There are moments in life when we need to burn the ships of our past. We do so by making a defining decision that eliminates the possibility of sailing back to the old world we left behind. You burn the ships named *Past Failure* and *Past Success*. You burn the ship named *Bad Habit*. You burn the ship named *Regret*. You burn the ship named *Guilt*.

That is precisely what Elisha did when he turned his plowing equipment into kindling and barbequed his oxen. It was his last supper. He said bye-bye to his old life by throwing a party for his friends. They shared a meal and stories into the wee hours. But it was the bonfire that made it the most meaningful and memorable night of his life because it symbolized the old Elisha. It was the last day of his old life and the first day of his new life.

Burning the plowing equipment was Elisha's way of burning the ships. He couldn't go back to his old way of life because he destroyed the stuff he *needed* to go back! Elisha the farmer was finished. This was the beginning of Elisha the prophet.

Stop and think about the symbolism of what Elisha did. Elisha literally cooked his old way of life and ate it for dinner. And forgive me if this is taking it too far, but after digesting it, he definitely got his "old ways" out of his system.

It doesn't matter whether you're trying to lose weight, get into a school or write a book. The first step is always the longest and the hardest. You wonder why you keep hooking up with your ex? Because you text her all day! Delete the dang number from your phone! You've got to eliminate the possibility of moving backward into the past.

That's how you go after goals.
That's how you break addictions.
That's how you reconcile relationships.
Burn 'em baby.

A New Chapter

When you began reading this chapter, chapter 6, you stopped reading the last chapter, chapter 5. That's how it works. You exited a chapter and entered into a new one. It's the same in life. We're stuck inside the boundaries of time, so things have to happen one after the other. And sometimes you need to begin a new chapter! How? With a simple punctuation mark. You can put a period on the page. It gets the job done. But if you want to be more dramatic, you can use an exclamation point. It's more decisive, definitive, final. Then you turn the page and begin a new sentence, which begins a new paragraph, which begins a new chapter. And even if the last chapter was short, you can still start a new one, even if you don't feel ready.

What's true in grammar is true in life! Not just because I'm a lover of grammar!

If you want to break a habit, stop a conflict, or just leave the past in the past, you need a punctuation mark. A comma won't cut it. Neither will a semicolon. You need a period or an exclamation point in your life!

Elisha didn't need to burn his plowing equipment to follow Elijah, but it made a statement. It was a hard statement of faith. No turning back there. If his internship with Elijah didn't pan out, he had no place else to turn. Which forced Elisha to *commit*.

This was Elisha's all in moment. Elisha wasn't just buying in. He was selling out! And that's what going *all in* is all about. You can't live too past tense or too future tense being all in. That doesn't mean you don't learn from the past or plan for the future, but you don't live there. Going all in is living like each day is the first day and last day of your life.

Have you made a statement of faith?

I'm not talking about repeating a sinner's prayer or taking con-firmation class. Come on. Those are fine, but they don't typically end with a bonfire and an oxen-cook. This has to be personal. A statement of faith has to make a statement.

Just please don't set fire to anything that doesn't belong to you. And don't copy someone else.

Think about it.

Pray about it.

Then *act* on it.

Make a Statement

Michael and Maria Durso are the founders of Christ Tabernacle in Queens, New York. Their spiritual journey started with some drama. In their twenties, Michael and Maria were as far from God as you can get. They mocked anything remotely religious. They were living together, living from drug fix to drug fix. Then one day Maria mysteriously came under the conviction of the Holy Spirit. She wasn't in church. She wasn't reading a Bible. She was in their hotel room on vacation. What she didn't know until she returned home is that a group of her friends had gotten saved while she was away. At that very moment, thousands of miles away, they were forming a prayer circle and interceding for Maria.

When they returned to New York, Michael and Maria stopped sleeping together and started going to church together. After making the decision to follow Christ, Michael knew he needed to cut himself from his past. He gathered all of his drug gear, maga-zines and videos that were representative of his old self. One by one, he dropped them down the incinerator chute of their NYC apartment building.

That's a statement of faith.

Remember the tax collector who put his faith in Christ?

He gave half of his possessions to the poor. His actions didn't save him, but the actions were a result of his being saved.

Remember the prostitute who anointed Jesus?

She broke open her alabaster jar. That isn't what saved her. But that dramatic action was evidence of a defining decision!

Remember what happened in Ephesus?

Sorcerers burned their scrolls publicly. The cumulative value of those scrolls was estimated at fifty thousand drachmas. A drachma was a silver coin worth a day's wages. That's 138 years of wages! They could've at least sold the scrolls and pocketed the money, but that' would have defeated the purpose. Instead they made a $3,739,972.50 worth of faith statements.

Past Tense

One of our biggest spiritual problems is this: we want God to do something new while we keep doing the same old thing. We want God to change our circumstances without us having to change at all. We're asking God for new wine, but we've still got an old wineskin.

Out with the old.

In with the new.

That's the essence of change. We get stuck, and sometimes *mad* at God, because we keep doing the same thing while expecting different results! Routines are a mighty important part of growth, but when the routine becomes routine, change it before you turn into a veggie. What got you to where you are might be holding you back from where God wants you to go next.

> *Seek me and live;*
> *do not seek Bethel,*
> *do not go to Gilgal,*
> *do not journey to Beersheba ...*
> *Seek the Lord and live.*

Bethel's the place where Jacob had his amazing dream. He built an altar there and made a promise. Gilgal is the place where the Israelites camped God on their first night in the Promised Land. By the way, it only took one night to get Israel out of Egypt, but it took forty years to get Egypt out of Israel. And Beersheba is where Abraham made a treaty with Abimelek and called on the Lord. His son Isaac dug a well and built an altar there.

All three places held special significance. They were sacred landmarks in Israel's spiritual journey. So why would God tell them not to seek Him there? The answer is simple: you won't find God in the past. His name is not *I Was*. His name is *I am*. If we obsess over what God did last, we'll miss what He wants to do next! God's at work right here, right now. God's always doing something brand spanking new! So go ahead and build altars to mark holy moments in the past, but the purpose of altars is to remind us of God's faithfulness in the past so we have the faith to believe in what He'll do next!

Press On

At some point in our lives, most of us stop living out of imagination and start living out of memory. That's the day we stop living and start dying. To be fully alive is to be fully present. And to do that, you've got to leave the past in the past. Paul says it best in Philippians 3:13 – 14:

> *Forgetting what is behind and straining toward what is ahead, I press on toward the goal to the win the prize for which God has called me heavenward in Christ Jesus.*

Press on indeed. That's gold!

Whenever I hear it, I have flashbacks to my college basketball days. There are two ways of playing defense. You can sit back in a half-court defense and let the other team come to you. It's a defensive way of playing the game. It's protecting the lead. It's playing not to lose. In football, it's called a prevent defense. But there is an offensive form of defense — the full-court press. You don't let the game come to you. You take it to them.

I'm afraid the church is content with a prevent defense while God is calling for a full-court press. We need to recapture the intensity of Matthew 11:12:

"From the days of John the Baptist until now, the kingdom of heaven has been forcefully advancing, and forceful men lay hold of it."

Are you playing offense in your dating? Or are you playing a prevent defense that leaves gentlemanliness, consideration, romance and respect on the sidelines? Are you relating reactively or proactively with your friends? Who's influencing who? Are you working for a paycheck or stewarding your God-given gifts pursuing a God-ordained dream? Are you trying to break even spiritually by avoiding sin? Or are you going for broke? I'll challenge you to go for broke. Carry the light with you everywhere! Love people just because.

At the end of every year, my wife and I take a little retreat to reflect on the past year and plan for the next one. We usually talk about our calendar and budget first. If we don't control our calendar, our calendar will end up controlling us. Budgeting is the way we play offense with our money. If you make your money work for you, no matter how much you have, it can't control you. I also check out my life goal list and set some new ones for the next calendar year. We walk away with an offensive game plan. Then on Mondays, which is my day off, Lora and I do a coffee date. It's a weekly touch point to make sure we're playing offense!

The only way to predict the future is to create it. You don't let it happen. You make it happen. How? Stop regretting the past and start learning from it. Let go of guilt and hurt by leaning into

God's grace. Quit beating yourself up and let the Spirit of God heal your heart. God wants to reconcile your past by redeeming it. He's in the recycling business: He makes recycled goods out of wasted lives.

Too many of us get comfortable with comfort. We follow Christ to the edge of inconvenience, but no further. That's when we need a friend to come slap us in the face and kick our butt over the edge!

Dancing Meadow

Elisha was a cool guy from a cool place called Abel Meholah. The English meaning is literally "meadow of dancing." His family had a pretty profitable farming operation going. Most family farms were small enterprises with a single plow and one set of oxen. Elisha's family had twelve yoke of oxen and farmhands to work them all, so they were well off. And it was all his to inherit. Burning the plowing equipment was more than quitting his job. He was writing himself out of the family will.

I think it's fair to say that Elisha was 200 percent committed to following Elijah. And that's what gave him the boldness to ask for a double portion of Elijah's anointing. And God granted it. During his sixty years of prophetic ministry, Elisha performed twenty-eight miracles as recorded in Scripture. That's exactly double the fourteen miracles that the prophet Elijah performed.

What gave Elisha the holy boldness to ask for double? I think it's the simple fact that he didn't withhold anything from God. And if you give all of yourself to God, you can ask and expect that God will give all of Himself to you because that's precisely what He wants to do. We have not because we ask not, and we ask not because we're not all in! If you ask for stuff constantly from your parents, then obviously you're going to hesitate before asking again, and they're going to hesitate before giving you more.

But if they *know* you're open with them, and obedient, well then you might have a deal.

Elisha could've lived his entire life in the dancing meadow. So can you. You can play it safe as long as you like. You'll just be a zombie, bored out of your mind. You can protect your reputation instead of risking it. You can save your money instead of giving it. You can keep plowing your fields instead of following the call of God, but you might very well be forfeiting twenty-eight miracles.

Double Anointing

One of the defining moments of my life happened when I was twenty-nine years old. I was sitting in a class at Regent University when a school administrator interrupted the class and told me my wife needed to speak to me. Nothing can prepare you to hear these words: "Mark, my dad died." It was easily the most shocking moment of my life.

Part of the reason for the shock is that my father-in-law was in the prime of life, the prime of ministry. Two days before his death, he'd had his annual physical, and the doctor had said, "You could drive a Mack Truck through your arteries." So how could he die of a heart attack forty-eight hours later?

We drove from Virginia Beach to DC in record time. We caught a flight to Chicago, where we met the rest of our family at the funeral home that evening. We had just been together for Christmas a week before, and my father-in-law was so full of life, so full of joy. To see his body in a casket was like a horrific dream. One we'd never wake up from.

Bob Schmidgall, my father-in-law, was my actual hero. He was an extremely gifted leader and teacher. I've never met anybody who prayed with more intensity and more consistency. He prayed *constantly*. At the time of his death, he was pastoring the same church (Calvary Church) he had started in 1967 with my mother-in-law. It was one of the largest and most generous churches in the country, giving millions of dollars to missions. I didn't even feel like a pastor compared to him. As I stood by the casket, I felt the Holy Spirit hovering over the chaos of our hearts. That's when I felt (the Holy Spirit gave me a little poke) like I should ask God for a double portion of my father-in-law's anointing. To be honest, I didn't know exactly what that even meant. I just knew I wanted his legacy to live on in me the way Elijah's legacy lived on in Elisha. And I think it does. The church I pastor still isn't as large as the church my father-in-law planted, but we have the same heartbeat. It's all about missions.

I'm very different from my father-in-law in gifting and personality. I'm called to write, for one. But I believe that even my writing anointing is an answer to the prayer I prayed by the casket. It's also an answer to the prayers my father-in-law prayed for me. His prayers did not die when he did. They live on long after his death. And just as God transferred the prophetic anointing from Elijah to Elisha, I believe that God somehow transferred my father-in-law's anointing to me.

Back to the Beginning

It's tough to rank the prophets, but if there were an ancient fantasy league in Israel, Elisha would be a first-round pick. Elisha gets some big points for parting the Jordan River, raising a boy from the dead, and making an iron axhead float. That's some serious fantasy points!

So why did God give Elisha a double portion?

For starters, Elisha asked for it. Then he backed it up by his willingness to go back to the beginning and start all over again. Elisha didn't hold out on God so God didn't hold out on Elisha. Elisha was all in.

Burning the plowing equipment was handing in his resignation as CEO of Elisha Farms, Inc. And Elisha gave it up for an unpaid internship with a crazy prophet whose name was almost the same. In one day he went from the top of the totem pole to the bottom. He got the jobs no one else wanted to do as an intern. But you have to be willing to climb the ladder, starting with the bottom rung.

Every black belt starts as a white belt.

Every musician starts with scales.

Every PhD starts in kindergarten.

If you aren't willing to begin at the beginning, God just can't use you. You're too thick. You've got to be willing to leave the seat of honor and take the lowest place at the table. You've got to be willing to go from first to last. Isn't that the example Jesus set? The all-powerful Creator became a servant. If you follow suit, there is nothing God can't do in you and through you.

Are you willing to start all over again?

Heather Zempel leads our small group ministry at NCC. She's a widely recognized leader in the discipleship world, as well as being a popular speaker and published author. I've never met anybody more passionate about spiritual formation. A decade ago, Heather was working on Capitol Hill for a US senator. She was using her environmental engineering degree to work on environmental policy and loving every minute of it. I threw down the gauntlet after she'd been attending NCC for a little while. I knew Heather had a leadership gift that God could use in the church, so I made an offer she couldn't refuse: more work for less money, and no office to go with it. Heather was willing to give up the prestige of working on Capitol Hill and all the perks that come with it to start all over again. She burned her ships. It was one of her all in moments. We only had two small groups at the time, but over the past decade she's raised up hundreds of leaders who create small group environments in which spiritual formation happens. She's engineered our free-market system of small groups that meet seven days a week all over the DC metro area. By free-market system, we simply mean that we let leaders get a vision from God and go for it.

That's how every success story begins in the kingdom of God. And by success, I simply mean stewarding your gifts to glorify God. In God's upside-down kingdom, a step down is a step up. And if you're willing to be demoted by men, then you're ready to be promoted by God Himself!

CHAPTER 7

CRASH
THE
PARTY

When one of the Pharisees invited Jesus to have
dinner with him, he went to the Pharisee's house
and reclined at the table. A woman in that town who
lived a sinful life learned that Jesus was eating at the
Pharisee's house, so she came there with an alabaster
jar of perfume. As she stood behind him at his feet
weeping, she began to wet his feet with her tears. Then
she wiped them with her hair, kissed them and poured
perfume on them.

Luke 7:36–38

The Bible's still got it! That thing's funny! There's some gold
situational comedy in there. And this is a classic. A party
hosted by a Pharisee? *Pharisee party*. Come on, that's classy
humor—I mean how fun could it have been? No deejay. No
punch. And definitely no pigs in blankets because that wouldn't
be kosher! The party favors were probably phylacteries! This is
the definition of "lame party."

Then in walks this woman.

Jesus had a twinkle in His eye, guaranteed. He knew it was

about to get offensive: the best kind of fun. If you follow in His footsteps, you'll eventually offend some Pharisees too.

Can you imagine the look on the Pharisees' stuck-up faces when this woman makes her surprise appearance? They start coughing uncontrollably when she busts out her jar of perfume. And then she starts wiping Jesus' feet with her hair.

Can you say *awkward*?

But she definitely made a statement, didn't she? Awkward moments like these are the spice of life!

This is one of the most intense, beautiful acts of worship and faith in all of Scripture. She risked her reputation — (what little she had left of it) — to honor Jesus. She *knew* the Pharisees stoned women like her, but that didn't keep her from just going for it. She used her most precious possession — an alabaster jar of perfume — to make her profession of faith. This stuff wasn't watered down, it was the real deal.

Break your Alabaster Jar

The alabaster jar of perfume was pure nard, a rare herb harvested in the Himalayas. This stuff is *powerful*. The jar itself was made of gems! This thing was her financial security — her most precious possession. And this is some beautiful irony: the perfume she used as a prostitute would become her profession of faith. She poured out every last drop at the feet of Jesus.

Breaking that bottle was her way of burning the ships. You can't hide stinky sin under sweet perfume forever. You have to let it out sometime. She walked out of the shadow of sin and into the light of the world.

We all need to come clean sooner or later. This is that moment for this woman.

Quit acting like sin disqualifies you from the grace of God. That's the *only* thing that qualifies us! Anything else is a fake, self-righteous attempt to "earn" God's grace. You can't *earn* God's grace.

Going all in means radical repentance. You have to fold. It begins by putting all of your cards face up on the table by confessing your sin to God. But remember that a halfhearted confession pretty much results in a halfhearted love for Christ. You need to come clean.

What would happen if we had this woman's courage, walked into a room full of self-righteous Pharisees, and revealed our sin unashamedly while anointing Jesus as Lord and Savior?

I know exactly what would happen: a revival on earth and a party in heaven.

Give it up

The alabaster jar is definitely one of the most unique offerings in Scripture. That's part of what made it so special and so personal. It was an intimate expression of love. Our church recently received a gift that falls in that same category.

It's a bittersweet story because of the deep pain in Shelley's heart. Her fiancé unexpectedly broke off their engagement. She felt like there was no way out of the prison of bitterness she found herself in, but that was when she felt prompted to give away what had once been her most precious possession — her engagement ring. She literally handed me the ring box and said, "God told me to give this to the church."

It was Shelley's statement of faith.

Then she preached a one-sentence sermon that was better than my best forty-minute message. She said, "I believe my act of obedience can turn into someone else's miracle."

And it did. It always does.

Matt started hanging out at NCC with his girlfriend, Jessica, during our *All In* series. As he listened to one of those messages,

Matt realized he had never defined his relationship with God. He wanted all God's benefits without any of the commitment. And that carried over into his relationship with Jessica. As Matt got more engaged at NCC, some mentors came into his life to call him out of his sin. Matt confessed his addiction to pornography, and it was a brand-new beginning. Confession kills the way sin makes you feel and heals the broken heart. Matt decided to go all in with God, and he began by moving out of the apartment he shared with Jess.

Matt wanted nothing more than to propose to Jess, but he needed to save enough money to buy a ring first. But as soon as he saved any money, an unexpected financial emergency drained his savings. It was right about the time that Matt was giving up on getting a ring for Jessica that Shelley gave her ring to NCC. We started praying that God would reveal the ones to whom the ring belonged, and it became pretty obvious that Matt's and Jessica's names were all over it.

Not long after we surprised Matt with the ring, he surprised Jessica. Matt pulled out the little black box while paddle boating on the Tidal Basin. He actually had a string tied to it because he was afraid he'd drop it in the water because he was shaking so bad! Matt managed to get down on one knee (it ain't so easy in a paddleboat) and popped the question. In that moment, Shelley's obedience turned into Matt and Jessica's miracle! It was Shelley's all in moment that made this all in moment possible.

One footnote.

Before Matt popped the question, he asked Jessica's dad if he could ask for his daughter's hand in marriage. Matt's father-in-law said, "All I've ever wanted for my children is that they would marry someone who loves Jesus first and foremost." Then he put Matt on the spot: "Matthew, can you tell me that you love Jesus more than Jessica?" Matt paused for a moment and then said, "For the first time in my life, I can honestly say yes."

What's most precious to you?

Your girlfriend or boyfriend? Your job? Your school? Your past accomplishments? Your future goals?

That's your alabaster jar of perfume, right there. And that needs smashing.

Let me shoot straight with you: Do you love Jesus more than your most precious possession? The most precious person in your life? Your deepest desire? Your greatest goal? Your proudest accomplishment?

Do you love Jesus first? Or second? Or third? Or tenth?

Minimum Wage

It's quite possible that the alabaster jar of perfume represented every penny of this woman's life savings. The rare value is evidenced by the fact that two gospel writers find it noteworthy enough to give us a written estimate: three hundred denarii — the equivalent of an entire year's salary! She didn't give Jesus minimum wage. She gave him top dollar!

I'll keep this one short and sweet because I didn't care much about money at your age, either. But you need to put your money where your mouth is no matter how much or how little of it you have! You may think it's easier to tithe if you make lots of money, but I think it's harder to tithe on minimum wage. Start now and it'll be easier when you get older.

I hope you're as inspired by this story as I am.

Standard of Giving

John Wesley is most famous for his open-air preaching, and the Methodist movement. But what I like about him was that he was an even better *giver* than he was a preacher! He lived by a simple motto: *Make all you can. Save all you can. Give all you can.*

Our family stole that motto, right there; it's gold! Every year we try to increase the percentage of income we give away. And John Wesley is a pretty good model for that. During his lifetime, Wesley gave away approximately 30,000 pounds (think British currency). Adjusted for inflation, that pans out to about $1,764,705.88 today!

Wesley's generosity came from a covenant he made with God in 1731. He decided to limit his expenses so he had more margin to give. His income ceiling was 28 pounds. That first year, John Wesley only made 30 pounds, so he gave just 2 pounds. The next year, his income doubled, and because he managed to continue living on 28 pounds, he had 32 pounds to give away! In the third year, his income increased to 90 pounds, but he kept his expenses flat.

Wesley's goal was to give away all excess income after bills were paid and family needs were taken care of. He never had more than 100 pounds in his possession because *he was afraid of storing up earthly treasure.* He believed that God's blessings should result in us raising our *standard of giving* and not our *standard of living.*

Wesley continued to raise his standard of giving. Even when his income was thousands and thousands of pounds, he lived simply and gave generously. He died with a few coins in his pocket but a storehouse of treasure in heaven. He was all in. It's obvious by the way he managed his money.

A Beautiful Thing

Your reactions say more about you than your actions. Most of us are good actors, but it's a little harder to fake a *reaction.* Look at the disciples' reactions when the woman busts open the alabaster jar. "Why this waste?" They thought this woman was pouring this perfume down the drain by pouring it at Jesus' feet. They were *offended* by it. But Jesus jumps to her defense. What they called a *waste* He called *a beautiful thing*. In fact, Jesus went so far as to say:

> "*Wherever this gospel is preached throughout the world, what she has done will also be told, in memory of her.*"

Think about what He just did for her self-image. You gotta love Jesus! I bet it had been years since she'd heard a single compliment like that. And that's a boss compliment! These words echoed in her mind for the rest of her life! And it turns out Jesus was right, because we're talking about her now!

Jesus wasn't going for fifteen minutes of fame. He prophesied that she would make His name famous all around the world with her one act of sacrifice! For this one act of going all in! Only a handful of history's most powerful and most influential people are still remembered. This *one* act of intense sacrifice says something about how *in* she was. She was all in!

No one can spot potential like Jesus. And that's because He gave it to us in the first place. Potential is God's gift to us. What we do with it is our gift back to God.

Live Up To

Johann Wolfgang von Goethe once said, "Treat a man as he is, and he will remain as he is. Treat a man as he can and should be, and he will become as he can and should be."

Is that true or what? Jesus gave this woman *something to live up to*. It's the exact opposite of what the Pharisees did. They murmured to each other, "If this man were a prophet, he would know who is touching him and what kind of woman she is — that she is a sinner."

The only thing the Pharisees saw when they looked at this woman was a sinner — nothing more.

I think Jesus saw an innocent little girl playing with her favorite doll — a little girl who had hopes and dreams that were nothing like the reality she was living. He sees past the past. He sees past the sin. He sees His image in us. God sees a reflection of Himself, in every little mirror He's created.

Pharisees treat people based on past performance.

Prophets treat people based on future potential.

Pharisees give people something to live down to.

Prophets give people something to live up to.

Pharisees write people off.

Prophets write people in.

Pharisees see sin.

Prophets see the image of God.

Pharisees give up on people.

Prophets give them a second chance.

The Pharisees reduced this woman to a label — sinner. Why do we do the same when Jesus specifically pointed out that the Pharisees are hypocrites? We give people political labels, sexual labels, and religious labels. But in the process, we strip them of their individual and awesome uniqueness. Prejudice is pre-judging. Judging before you even know how much potential someone has. According to God, it's a lot.

God just can't give up on you. It's not in His nature. His goodness and mercy will follow you every day of your life.

Desperados

I think it's safe to say this prostitute was *not* on the guest list. That I'm sure of. But she was probably pretty good at getting in and out of back doors. She really could've just waited, but she decided to crash the party.

Jesus didn't have the time of day for religiosity. Religious protocol meant nothing to Him. If it did, He would have chosen the Pharisees as His disciples. Instead, Jesus chose those desperate enough to take desperate measures! Think of them as spiritual desperadoes.

Jesus honored the tax collector who climbed a sycamore tree in a three-piece suit just to get a glimpse of Jesus. He honored the four friends who climbed up and cut a hole in someone's ceiling by healing their paralyzed friend. He honored the woman who fought her way through the crowds just to touch the hem of His garment. And Jesus honored this prostitute who crashed the party.

Nothing's changed. God is still honoring desperados who climb trees, fight crowds, and crash parties. How desperate are you? Desperate enough to go all in with God?

True spirituality is "the place where desperation meets Jesus."

The easiest and shortest way *never* gets us where we want to go. Shortcuts always end up being failures. The willingness to go out of your way for God is what'll make you grow. You'll find God in uncomfortable places at inconvenient times. But if you go out of your way for God, God will go out of His way for you.

Crash a party!

CHAPTER 8

RIM
HUGGERS

Of all the life goals I've knocked out, hiking the Grand Canyon from rim to rim with my son Parker is at the top of the list. It was the magical combination of ridiculously difficult and ridiculously beautiful. I really don't think I've ever done anything more physically demanding, but that is what made it so memorable. It took an all-out effort to come out on the other side.

My first glimpse of the Grand Canyon through the giant window at the Grand Canyon Lodge was unforgettable. I stood and stared for an hour. Next to my wife walking down the aisle on our wedding day, no image has left a more permanent imprint on my brain. To simply call the Grand Canyon one of the seven natural wonders of the world seems like geological blasphemy. When the sunrise paints the western wall in pink and purple, it's like seeing the Creator's reflection.

I've done some intense hikes, over longer periods of time, but those challenges weren't nearly as difficult or dangerous as crossing 23.2 miles of canyon in two days, with a one-mile descent and ascent in elevation in 110 degree temperatures! I lost thirteen pounds in two days! Trust me, there are much safer ways to lose weight than "the Grand Canyon workout."

Our predawn descent down the North Kaibab Trail *pounded* me, but I was a little more concerned about the safety of my twelve-year-old son. I thought we had more than enough water in our packs, but we ran out and cramped up three miles before reaching our day-one destination. I kept monitoring Parker, "How are you doing on a scale of 1 to 10?" The number kept dropping until he said, "Negative one!" That's when I wondered if we were the overconfident hikers the park rangers had warned us about (the ones who get airlifted out by helicopter).

When we arrived at Phantom Ranch on the canyon floor around dusk, we felt like a car rolling into a gas station on fumes. We had just enough energy to eat dinner and collapse into bed. When my alarm went off at four-thirty the next morning, I felt paralyzed. We chose the shorter, steeper route out of the canyon with about 120,000 switchbacks on the final leg. Oops!

As we zigzagged our way up the Bright Angel Trail, we could see hundreds of sightseers lining the South Rim. They were as mesmerized by its majesty as we had been the day before. And that's when the contrast struck me. Our clothes were caked with orange canyon clay mixed with salty sweat stains. Flies hovered. The sightseers who lined the rim were wearing brand-spanking-new souvenir T-shirts from a *gift shop*. We were absolutely parched and scorched. They looked like they had just emerged from their air-conditioned hotel rooms — some were licking ice cream cones.

For a split second, I felt sorry for myself. Then I felt sorry for them. Because they were *seeing it* and *missing it* at the same time. You can't truly see what you haven't personally experienced. People who stand and stare, but never hike into the canyon are what I like to call rim-huggers.

When Parker and I reached the South Rim, the first thing we did was turn around and look at the trail we had just spanked. We stood right next to rim huggers with the very same view, but they didn't appreciate it like we did. They couldn't. They were *seeing* it, but we had *experienced* it. Hikers know the canyon in a way that huggers never will!

Here's the point: there is a world of difference between *knowing about God* and *knowing God*. The difference between those two things is the distance between the North Rim and South Rim, with the canyon in between.

That's when this thought crossed my mind: *most Christians are rim huggers!*

We Don't Get Credit for an Audit

We all want to spend *eternity* with God. We just don't want to spend *time* with Him. We sit and stare from a distance — satisfied with superficiality. We Facebook more than we seek His face. And our eyes aren't fixed on Jesus—they're plastered to our iPhones and iPads — emphasis on "i." Then, we wonder why God feels so distant. It's because we're hugging the rim. We wonder why we're bored with our faith. It's because we're holding out! We want joy without sacrifice. We want character without suffering. We want success without failure. We want gain without pain. We want a testimony without the test. Are you starting to see what's wrong with that?

God is like a Grand Canyon. In the words of A. W. Tozer, "Eternity will not be long enough to learn all He is, or to praise Him for all He has done." But you don't get to know God by looking at Him from a distance. You have to hike into the depths of His power and the heights of His holiness. You have to go rim to rim with God. And if you take a single Spirit-led step of faith in God's direction, spiritual adrenaline will surge through your veins once again.

Sitting in a church service for sixty minutes does squat. Don't get me wrong, going to church is a good thing, a biblical thing, the right thing. But I'll tell you right now that you don't do anybody any favors by just sitting there. Churches are filled with spiritual sightseers who feel like they've done their religious duty by sitting and listening. We don't get credit for an audit. That's not quite how it works. Stop letting someone else worship for you, study for you, fast for you, journal for you and pray for you.

That's when church attenders become rim huggers.

Are you a hugger or a hiker?

Take a Hike

This year, our church will take twenty-five mission trips. Our goal is fifty-two trips a year so that a mission team is coming and going all the time. Mission trips turn huggers into hikers! One mission trip is worth a lot more than fifty-two sermons!

We're already educated way beyond the level of our obedience. We don't need another sermon. Please don't misinterpret what I'm saying — we need to study God's Word diligently. But we don't need to know more. We need to do more with what we know. At the end of the day, God isn't going to say, "Well thought, Intellectual." He'll say one thing and one thing only: "Well done, good and faithful servant!"

In the Hebrew language, there's no distinction between *knowing* and *doing*. Knowing is doing and doing is knowing. In other words, if you aren't doing it, then you don't really know it. You're a rim hugger.

Take a hike!

It's time to go all in by going all out. The phrase "all out" simply means giving God 100%. It's giving God everything you've got. It's all about loving God with *all* your heart, soul, mind, and strength. It's not just worshiping God with words during a nice emotional worship session, it's worshiping God with blood, sweat, and tears.

You can't be the hands and feet of Jesus if you're sitting on your butt.

Church isn't a spectator sport. Church isn't even a building with an address. Church isn't a gathering at a certain time. If you *are* the church, then "church" is happening whenever and wherever you are.

Your school is your mission field.

Your life is your sermon.

Your friends are your congregation.

That's why we often end our services with this closing:

When you leave this place, you don't leave the presence of God. You take the presence of God with you wherever you go.

CHAPTER 9

CLIMB
THE
CLIFF

Saul was staying on the outskirts of Gibeah under a
pomegranate tree in Migron. With him were about six
hundred men.

1 Samuel 14:2

I was recently on a flight from Ethiopia to DC. I got tired of
reading, so I flipped on the film, *We Bought a Zoo*. Based on a
true story, Matt Damon plays the role of a writer, Benjamin Mee,
who rescues a failing zoo while coming to terms with his life (his
wife has died and he's a single father). One line from the film
is unforgettable: "Sometimes all you need is twenty seconds of
insane courage." That's awesome. And true! Twenty seconds can
change the plot of your whole life.

Twenty seconds of insane courage.

Think about it! Twenty seconds: that's it. That's about how long it
took for Peter to get out of the boat in the middle of the Sea of Galilee. That's about how long it took for David to charge Goliath. That's
about how long it took for Zacchaeus to climb the sycamore tree.

History turns on a dime, and the dime is a decision that takes
twenty seconds of *insane* courage. That's about how long it took

for me to hand my life over to Jesus. That's about how long it took for me to call my wife, Lora, to ask her out on our first date! That's about how long it took to say *yes* to a church plant in Washington, DC. That last one might've been closer to thirty seconds ... but regardless!

Twenty seconds of insane courage.

I'm telling you, that's all it takes.

What difficult decision do you need to make?

What tough conversation do you need to have?

What crazy risk do you need to take?

Holy Crazy

Sometimes one snapshot of one moment of one person's life is a caricature of a person's entire character. This is that moment for Saul. Can't you see Saul snacking on seeds while reclining in the shade of a pomegranate tree? I bet some of the lowest-ranking privates were even fanning him! Instead of picking a fight with some bad guys, the leader of Israel's army is picking *pomegranates*. And he drags his whole army along with him. No surprises here either — Saul has a long history of letting others fight his battles for him. Saul was a rim hugger. But his son Jonathan was a cliff climber.

Saul was playing not to lose. Jonathan was playing to *win*. That's the difference between fear and faith. If you let fear dictate your decisions, you'll live defensively, reactively, and cautiously. Living by faith is playing offense with your life.

Twenty seconds of insane courage.

I can't think of a better description than Jonathan picking a fight with the Philistines. All of them. It was crazy, but if God's in it, it's *holy* crazy.

Don't be surprised if people mock you and laugh at you when you do something crazy. People are jealous and fearful by nature. Get over it and get on with it. People may think you're crazy when you climb a cliff, but you can be crazy or you can be normal. Who wants to be normal? Me either!

I'm sure the other eleven disciples made flailing motions to Peter, mocking him for sinking in the Sea of Galilee, but *they* never walked on water, did they? Have you ever noticed how most people who criticize people like Peter do so from the comfortable confines of a boat? And most people who criticize cliff climbers do so from the bottom of a mountain with a pair of binoculars.

David's brothers laid into him for challenging Goliath, but David made headlines while his brothers sat on the sidelines! And I'm sure the crowd got a kick out of a tax collector climbing a tree to get a glimpse of Jesus, but *they* didn't get invited to lunch with Jesus.

So what motivated Jonathan to climb the cliff? What triggered the twenty seconds of insane courage? Let me set the scene.

During the early days of Saul's kingship, the Philistines controlled the western border of Israel and battle lines were drawn at a place called Mikmash. Saul seemed fine sitting on the sideline, but Jonathan wanted to be on the front line.

"Come, let's go over to the Philistine outpost on the other side."

Going all out for God always starts with one step of faith. It's often the longest, hardest, and scariest step. But when we make a move that is motivated by God's glory, it moves the heart and hand of God.

There comes a moment in our lives when enough is enough. The pain of staying the same is greater than the pain of change. We reject the status quo. We refuse to remain the same.

This is that moment for Jonathan.

The New Living Translation captions it "Jonathan's Daring Plan." To be perfectly honest, it seems like a dumb plan. It has to rank as the worst military strategy ever. Jonathan exposes himself to the enemy in broad daylight and hands over the high ground. Then he comes up with this sign to determine whether or not to attack:

"But if they say, 'Come up to us,' we will climb up, because that will be our sign that the LORD has given them into our hands."

If I'm making up the signs, I do the exact opposite! If *they* come down to us, that'll be our sign. Or better yet, if they fall off the cliff, that'll be our sign. Jonathan chooses the most difficult and dangerous option. To the rest of us, this isn't really an option. But when did we start believing that Jesus died to keep us safe? God's plan isn't an insurance plan.

I'm not sure which was more dangerous — climbing the cliff or fighting the Philistines. There's no guarantee that Jonathan would even survive the climb. It's not like the Philistines dropped a rope. And even if he made it to the top, Jonathan and his armor-bearer were outnumbered like a hundred to one.

I went rock climbing once, and my hands were clenched in a claw-like position for several hours afterward. Can you imagine sword fighting after climbing a cliff? But he's not looking for the easy way out. It's a legit all-out assault. He's not taking the path of least resistance, he's taking the most difficult path possible. Jonathan was the underdog, big-time, and he knew that if he pulled off this upset, God would get tons of glory!

So what motivated Jonathan? What triggered the twenty seconds of insane courage?

It's impossible to psychoanalyze someone who lived thousands of years ago, but one statement reveals Jonathan's MO. It's the key code in his operating system. And it's easily one of my favorite sentences in the whole Bible. It's even our philosophy of ministry at NCC. One statement reveals everything I need to know about Jonathan.

"Perhaps the LORD will act in our behalf."

I think most of the doubters of the world think the opposite: perhaps the Lord *won't* act in our behalf. They let fear make their decisions for them instead of faith! Lame! And they wonder how they end up under a pomegranate tree on their butts.

Our lack of guts is really a lack of faith. Instead of playing to win, we play not to lose. But cliff climbers would rather fall on their face than sit on their butt. They'd rather make mistakes than miss opportunities. Cliff climbers know that one step of faith brings out the big guns: God! That's precisely what happened because of Jonathan's bold move.

So on that day the LORD saved Israel.

All it took was one daring decision! That's really all it ever takes. Regrets of *not* making the climb will haunt you till the day you die, I can promise you that.

But this day could be *that day*. And all it ever takes is one defining decision. I'm going to keep drilling it: it only takes twenty seconds.

I recently spoke at a college commencement. Let me share the manifesto I shared with them. It's all about going all in and going all out for God.

Quit living as if the purpose of life is to arrive safely at death.
Set God-sized goals. Pursue God-ordained passions. Go after a
dream that is destined to fail without divine intervention.
Keep asking questions. Keep making mistakes.
Keep seeking God.
Stop pointing out problems and become part of the solution.
Stop repeating the past and start creating the future.
Stop playing it safe and start taking risks.
Expand your horizons. Accumulate experiences.
Enjoy the journey.
Find every excuse you can to celebrate everything you can.
Live like today is the first day and last day of your life.
Don't let what's wrong with you keep you from worshiping
what's right with God.

Burn sinful bridges. Blaze new trails.
Don't let fear dictate your decisions. Take a flying leap of faith.
Quit holding out. Quit holding back.
Go all in with God. Go all out for God.

Pick a Fight

I have a friend, Bob Goff, who's full of whimsy. That's a nice way of saying that he's actually crazy. And Bob would be the first to admit it and be flattered by your pointing it out. If you haven't read his book *Love Does*, you need to. We had dinner one night after he spoke at NCC, and Bob told us to *take over a country*! He wasn't kidding! With a grin on his face, he said, "Why not?" And why wouldn't Bob challenge us, after the way God used this one crazy dude to influence Uganda? More on that in a minute.

If you know me, you know I use a lot of "there are two types of people in this world …" statements. But this is for real! There are two kinds of people in the world (really) — those who ask *why* and those who ask *why not*. *Why* people look for excuses. *Why not* people look for opportunities! *Why* people are afraid of making mistakes. *Why not* people don't want to miss out on God-ordained opportunities! I don't know about you, but I'd much rather hang out with a *why not* person, which kind of makes me want to *be* one … Food for thought.

I first met Bob at the National Prayer Breakfast in Washington, DC. He was on a panel dealing with human trafficking. Through a classic, crazy series of events, Bob was named honorary consul for the Republic of Uganda to the United States. And he's a US citizen. Go figure.

Much of Bob's work in Uganda involves fighting for those who can't fight for themselves. Every year, witch doctors kill hundreds of children as ritual sacrifices (that still exists)!? A little boy named Charlie was supposed to be one of them, but despite being brutally disfigured, he managed to escape with his life. Bob prosecuted and got the very first conviction against a witch doctor in the history of the country. He also became friends with Charlie! He flew Charlie to the US, where he could get the surgery he needed, and secured a scholarship so Charlie can get a college education when that day arrives.

It was during that panel discussion that Bob made an offhanded comment that has become a personal mantra: *pick a fight*. That statement sort of rocked me.

That's exactly what Jonathan did! He decided to pick a fight with the Philistines. He was sick of backing down, so he stood up. Why play defense when you can play *offense*? Much more fun.

How do we pick a fight?

It starts when we get on our knees. Prayer is picking a fight with the Enemy, and that's where the battle's won or lost. Prayer is the difference between us fighting for God and God fighting for us. But we can't just hit our knees. We also have to take a step, take a stand. So pray until you've gotten over yourself, and then follow where God leads you! Pick a fight with who He tells you to, for Bob it was a witch doctor.

Here's the rest of the story.

After booking the witch doctor, Bob visited him in prison. That witch doctor gave his life to Jesus and is now preaching the gospel to other prisoners. That's what can happen when we pick a fight with the Enemy! It's not about winning a battle — it's about getting everyone on God's side!

Play Offense

I think we've conveniently forgotten that we were born in the middle of a battlefield. Good and evil are in constant conflict all around us. But Jesus' call to arms was also a promise:

"I will build my church, and the gates of Hades will not overcome it."

Gates are defensive tools. That means, by definition, we should be playing offense! And being offensive! Faithfulness isn't holding down the fort, it's storming the gates of hell and taking back enemy territory that belongs to God.

NCC doesn't sit still for very long. We have a little motto that says: *Go. Set. Ready.* That may seem backward, but it's the way we keep moving forward. If we wait till we're ready, we'll be waiting the rest of our lives.

Two thousand years ago, Jesus pretty much said *go*. We've got the green light. Do you need to make sure it's the will of God? Of course you do. But always continue growing and moving forward.

I try to live my personal life the same way our church does. That's why I'm a big believer in life goals. We won't accomplish any goals we don't set. Goals are dreams with targets on them. And once we set them, it keeps us on the offensive.

You can let fear dictate your decisions or you can let faith dictate your decisions. Who or what you allow to dictate will ultimately determine whether you're a rim hugger or a cliff climber. Tell your fears to sit down and shut up in Jesus' name every time they hold you back from doing God's will, God's work.

Better Safe than Sorry

It's important to recognize the difference between *personality* issues and *spiritual* issues. We all have a different risk threshold, meaning some people seem to be wired for risk, and others just aren't. And a small risk for someone with a low tolerance for risk is a huge risk for him or her.

Think of it this way. There are spiritual gifts like mercy, faith, or generosity that enable people to *set the standard*. But just because you don't have that spiritual gift doesn't mean you aren't held to any standard at all. Even if you aren't gifted in that way, you should still live mercifully, faithfully, and generously. You might not *set the standard*, but you need to *meet the standard*. Also, don't justify being a jerk with your gift. I've met too many people who say things like "I'm super honest" to justify talking about someone in a mean way. Please don't be that "blunt" person who's really just rude. Speak the truth in love.

A pair of psychologists from the University of Michigan did a study a decade ago that reframed the way I think about fear. Researchers monitored brain activity in response to winning and losing during a computer-simulated betting game. Researchers came to a simple yet profound conclusion: *losses loom larger than gains*. In other words, losing hurts a lot more than winning feels good.

Maybe that helps explain why so many people play to not lose. It's our brain's default setting. It's why we approach God's grand plans with a "better safe than sorry" mentality. We're so afraid of making the wrong decision that we make no decision. And no decision is a decision. It's called indecision. And it's a wrong decision.

Take a Stand

On October 31, 1517, a monk named Martin Luther picked a great fight. He attacked the selling of indulgences. Indulgences were sold by the Catholic Church, and could "erase" a sin or reduce your time in "purgatory." Luther posted ninety-five reasons why they were dead wrong on the doors of All Saints' Church in Wittenberg, Germany, and ignited the Protestant Reformation.

I actually visited Wittenberg a few years ago *on* Reformation Day. What I love about the story is how a little-known monk in a tiny town in the middle of nowhere could impact history the way he did. But that's what happens when you go *all in*.

I don't think Martin Luther knew he was making history as he made history, but our small acts of courage can have a domino effect. All we need to do is stand up, step in, or step out.

Holy Roman emperor Charles V put the poor guy on trial in 1521, but Martin refused to back down: "My conscience is taken captive by God's Word, I cannot and will not recant anything. For to act against our conscience is neither safe for us, nor open to us. On this I take my stand. I can do no other. God help me. Amen."

Let me bring it a little closer to home.

Who do you need to stand up for? The homeless? The fatherless? The voiceless? Stop reading for a minute and actually think about that. Maybe it's a friend or issue you care about deeply. Step up and make a difference!

It may feel like an overwhelming problem or challenge or dream, but don't let what you can't do keep you from doing what you can. Take the first step! Climb the cliff. Pick the fight.

Perhaps the Lord will act in your behalf . . .

CHAPTER 10

BUILD THE ARK

> By faith Noah, when warned about things not yet seen, in holy fear built an ark to save his family.
>
> Hebrews 11:7

In 1948, Korczak Ziolkowski was commissioned by a Lakota Chief (named Henry Standing Bear) to design a mountain carving that would honor the famous war leader Crazy Horse. The great irony is that Crazy Horse didn't even allow himself to be photographed! You have to wonder how he'd feel about a 563-foot-high statue of himself carved in the granite face of the Black Hills. Ziolkowski spent more than three decades of his life carving the epic statue that's eight feet taller than the Washington Monument and nine times larger than the faces on Mount Rushmore. Since Korczak's death in 1982, the Ziolkowski family has carried on their father's vision and continued carving. Their projected date of completion is 2050, just shy of the one-hundred-year mark.

One hundred years devoted to one task!

It's hard to imagine, isn't it? But Crazy Horse falls twenty years short of how long it took Noah to build the ark. Noah's ark project ranks as one of history's largest and longest construction projects! I think we fail to appreciate it for what it is — a really big boat built a really long time ago! And they didn't have power tools back then like we do today!

The ark measured 300 cubits in length, 50 cubits in width, and 30 cubits in height. In the Hebrew system of measurement, a cubit was the equivalent of 17.5 inches. That means the ark was the length of one and a half football fields! Not until the late nineteenth century did a ship that size get constructed again. Yet even today, the 30:5:3 design ratio is still considered the golden mean ratio for stability during storms at sea. The internal volume of the ark was 1,518,750 cubit feet — the equivalent of 569 boxcars. If the average animal was the size of a sheep, it had capacity for 125,000 animals. To put that into perspective, there are only 2,000 animals from 400 different species at the National Zoo in Washington, DC. That means you could fit 60 National Zoos on board Noah's ark!

Building the ark required a rare combination of brains and brawn. This thing was the first boat ever built. It's not like it came with an instruction manual. It was also backbreaking work. It took buckets of blood, sweat, and tears. But even more than brains and brawn, it took some *insane* faith to build this beast.

Who builds a boat in the desert? Who hammers away for 120 years at something they might not even need? He based his entire future on something that had never happened before.

According to Jewish tradition, Noah didn't just start building the ark. He planted trees first. After they were fully grown, he cut down the trees, sawed them into planks, and built the boat!

That's going all out for God. Noah obviously wasn't after fifteen minutes of fame, he was after eternal glory.

Long Obedience

Toward the end of his life, Korczak Ziolkowski talked a little about his artistic passion, and simply said, "When your life is over, the world will ask you only one question: 'Did you do what you were supposed to do?'"

That's better than a good question, that's *the* question! *Did you do what you were supposed to do?*

You can't answer that question with words, only with your life!

Noah built the ark because God commanded it. It's what he was supposed to do. When everything was said and done, it was the longest act of obedience recorded in the entire Bible. From start to finish, Noah's one act of obedience took 43,800 days. That's probably *the* hardest single job God's given anyone in the entire Bible. If I had to take anyone's place in the Bible, Noah would probably be dead last on my list! Just being honest!

I'm know what I'm supposed to do: write books. I actually scored below average on an aptitude exam for writing when I was in graduate school, but I *knew* I was called to write. And my lack of "aptitude" just means I have to rely on God even more when I write. For thirteen years, I was a frustrated writer. I couldn't complete even one manuscript. When I finally published my first book, *In a Pit with a Lion on a Snowy Day*, I felt more relief than joy. I knew I had finally done exactly what I was supposed to do.

Writing is a lot more than combinations of words and sentences and paragraphs and chapters. For me, writing a book is an act of obedience that takes like six months of early mornings and late nights.

I don't write with a keyboard. I pray with it.

Setting my alarm for early in the morning and sitting down at my keyboard are acts of obedience. It's what I'm supposed to do. The harder it is and the longer it takes, the more God is glorified! The more He's pleased.

No matter what tool your tool is — a football, some sheet music, a hammer, a keyboard, a mop, a microphone, or an espresso machine — using it is an act of obedience! It's the mechanism whereby you worship God. It's the way you do what you're supposed to do.

I love the way Dr. Martin Luther King Jr. put it:

> *If it falls your lot to be a street sweeper, sweep streets like Michelangelo painted pictures, like Shakespeare wrote poetry, like Beethoven composed music; sweep streets so well that all the host of heaven and earth will have to pause and say, "Here lived a great street sweeper, who swept his job well."*

The Point of Precedence

It might be getting old at this point, but I love imagining what was going through people's heads in the Bible! For Noah, I'm guessing it was either *You've got to be kidding* or *You've got to be crazy!* He probably woke up every morning and questioned his sanity. But he obeyed anyway. Enough said!

> *Noah did everything just as God commanded him.*

I don't know about you, but I always wish God would reveal the second step before I take the first step (the one that requires faith). But I've discovered that if I don't take the first step, God's not going to just let you have the second one. This is why we get stuck spiritually. We want more revelation before we obey more, but God wants more obedience before He reveals more. Or we want God to lay out some optional plans and then let us pick our favorite. But that's not quite how it works!

Most of us will only follow Christ to a place where we've been before. But no further. None of that unfamiliar territory business! And as a result, we give up all the new gifts, new anointings, and new dreams that God has waiting for us.

If you want God to do something new, you can't keep doing what you've always done. Push past the fear of the unknown. You've obviously got to do something different!

It seems appropriate to use an animal illustration — Noah *was* the world's first zoologist after all. The African impala is famous for its crazy leaping ability. It can jump ten feet high and thirty feet forward. You'd think zookeepers would have a tough time keeping impalas in their enclosures, but they have a little trick. A three-foot wall does the trick, because an impala won't jump if it can't see where it will land.

We have the same problem, right? We want a money-back guarantee before we do *anything*, but that eliminates faith from the equation. Sometimes we need to take a flying leap of faith!

We need to step into the conflict without knowing if we can resolve it. We need to share our faith without knowing how our friends will react to it. We need to pray for a miracle without knowing how God will answer. We need to put ourselves in a situation that activates a spiritual gift we've never exercised before. And we need to go after a dream that'll fail without divine intervention.

If you want to discover new lands, you'll have to lose sight of the shore. Have you ever seen a movie or heard a song that's super *predictable*? Boring, right? We've got to sail past the predictable. And when we do, we develop a spiritual hunger for the miraculous and lose our appetite for the habitual. We also get a little taste of God's favor, which makes the usual taste like dirt.

Found Favor

Noah found favor in the eyes of the Lord.

In a time when great wickedness was all over the earth, one man stood out. The favor of God came to Noah because he was righteous when nobody else was. Let me define *favor* for you:

it's what God can do for you that you cannot do for yourself. It's His favor that opens the door of opportunity, and turns enemies into friends. I pray for the favor of God more than anything else. I pray it for my books, for National Community Church, and I pray it for my children. I've prayed it (based on Luke 2:52) for my children a million times:

May you grow in wisdom and stature, and in favor with God and man.

So how do you find favor? You know the answer by now don't you? Obedience.

It starts by surrendering our lives to the lordship of Jesus Christ. Jesus proclaimed the favor of God in His very first sermon. Then He sealed the deal with His death and resurrection. Favor is a function of surrender. If we don't hold out on God, God won't hold out on us!

No good thing does God withhold from those who walk uprightly.

We position ourselves for the favor of God with humility and obedience.

All we really need is the favor found at the foot of the cross. But the favor of God is not limited to the spiritual realm, it also extends into the material realm as well. In Noah's life, it translated into some novel inventions. He was the Leonardo da Vinci and Thomas Edison of his era! Noah didn't just build the first ship. According to Jewish tradition, Noah also invented the plow, the scythe, the hoe, and a number of other implements used for cultivating the ground. The favor of God translated into brilliant God-ideas.

It doesn't matter what you do, God wants to help you do it. Your desires can be the Lord's desires as well — for your game, your recital, your film, or your exams. But you've got to position yourself for that favor by acting in obedience. That's when He can bless you beyond your ability and resources.

If You Build It

One of my all-time favorite movie lines is from *Field of Dreams*. I know 1989 might be a little before your time, but in it Kevin Costner plays novice farmer and baseball-lover Ray Kinsella. While walking through a cornfield, Ray hears a faint whisper: "If you build it, they will come." Ray literally quits farming and builds a baseball diamond in the middle of nowhere. And sure enough, the ghosts of baseball past appear and play ball!

About a decade ago, I had a kind of "field of dreams" moment. In my case, it wasn't a cornfield in Iowa. It was a *crack house* on Capitol Hill. One day as I walked by a junked property that I had passed hundreds of times before, I heard the still small voice of the Holy Spirit: *This crack house would make a great coffeehouse.* It's not easy to tell all the time, but I was pretty sure this was a God-idea.

The original asking price for the property was $1 million because it's less than five blocks from the Capitol, and one block from Union Station. After circling it in prayer for years, we eventually got it for $325,000.

Churches don't usually build coffeehouses, but Jesus hung out at wells, not just synagogues. So even though we felt as foolish as Noah building the ark, we knew that if we built it people would come. And they have — we have about 600 customers per day. And Ebenezer's coffeehouse has been voted the number one coffeehouse in the metro DC area.

Faith is the willingness to look foolish. Noah looked a little dumb building a boat in the desert. Sarah looked foolish buying maternity clothes at *ninety*. Moses looked pretty stupid asking Pharaoh to let his slaves go. The Israelite army looked foolish marching around Jericho blowing horns. David probably seemed awfully dense coming at Goliath with a dinky slingshot. The Wise Men didn't *seem* so smart following a star to who knows where.

Peter looked foolish stepping out of the boat in the middle of the lake in the middle of the night. And everyone thought Jesus was dead wrong when He died on the cross. But the results speak for themselves, don't they?

Noah stayed afloat during the flood. Sarah gave birth to Isaac. Moses delivered Israel out of Egypt. The walls of Jericho came tumbling down. David defeated Goliath. The Wise Men found the Messiah. Peter walked on water. And Jesus rose from the dead.

People are afraid to look stupid, and that's stupid! That's also why so many people have never built an ark, killed a giant, or walked on water.

Since writing *The Circle Maker*, I've gotten a million emails from people sharing prayer testimonies with me. One of my favorites talks about a drought fifty years ago. An entire season of crops was just about dead and gone when a rural Mississippi church made up of farming families called an emergency prayer meeting. Dozens of farmers showed up to pray. All of them wore their overalls, except for one farmer, who wore waders. He got a few funny looks, a bit like Noah. But isn't that just pure, straight-up faith? If you genuinely believe God will answer your prayer for rain, isn't that exactly what you would wear? Dress for the miracle! I love the childlike faith of that seasoned farmer. He simply said, "I don't want to walk home wet." And he didn't. But everyone else did!

I can't help but wonder if that one act of faith is what sealed the deal. I don't know for sure, but I do know that faith is acting *as if* God has already answered. And acting *as if* God has answered means acting on our prayers, even if it takes 120 years.

Keep Hammering Away

We don't really stop to think about what life on the ark was like, but I think it's safe to say that Noah didn't get much sleep. He was feeding, cleaning, and caring for thousands of animals around the clock. And it must've smelled to high *heaven*. African elephants alone produce eighty pounds of waste per *day*. It was smelly and messy. That right there is a pretty good picture of what obedience looks like.

The blessings of God will complicate your life, but unlike sin, they will complicate your life in the way it should be complicated. Marrying Lora complicated my life. Praise God. We have three complications named Parker, Summer, and Josiah. National Community Church is far more complicated now than it was when we had nineteen people!

No matter what vision God has given you, I can predict it will *take longer* and *be harder* than you ever imagined. But Noah offers a little reality check, doesn't he? If a decade sounds like a long time to patiently pursue a God-ordained passion, try twelve of them! It's amazing what God can do if you keep hammering away for 120 years! We overestimate what we can do in a year, but we underestimate what God can do in a decade.

Living for God isn't just about getting where He wants you to go. It's about who you become in the process. And it's not about how quickly you get there: it's about how far you go.

Going all out is going the *distance*.

It's crossing the finish line the way the apostle did:

I have fought the good fight, I have finished the race, and I have remained faithful.

CHAPTER 11

GRAB
YOUR
OXGOAD

After Ehud came Shamgar son of Anath, who struck
down six hundred Philistines with an oxgoad. He too
saved Israel.

Judges 3:31

In 1963, Edward Lorenz theorized that a minor event like the
flapping of a butterfly's wing in Brazil could conceivably alter
wind currents sufficiently to cause a tornado in Texas. His theory
took off in the academic community and became known to the
general public as *the butterfly effect*.

The theory was the result of a computer program that Lorenz
designed to be able to forecast weather. On the day of his acci-
dental discovery, Lorenz had to hurry out of his office for a meeting. Instead of entering a number he used on previous trials, he
rounded it up. Lorenz figured that a change of one one-thou-
sandth of 1 percent would be inconsequential. He figured wrong.
He came back and the tiny change simulated a massively catastrophic event in weather. According to Lorenz, the numerical
difference between the original number and the rounded number

was the equivalent of a puff of wind, but the net difference was the equivalent of a catastrophic weather event.

Lorenz came to a simple conclusion: *minuscule changes in input can make a huge difference in output.*

It's true in science. It's true in life!

That simple discovery can totally change your life. It can radically alter your spiritual, emotional, relational, or financial forecast. It can change the atmosphere in your studies, job, and friendships.

You don't have to make one hundred changes. All that does is divide your energy by one hundred and results in a 1 percent chance of success. You have to be 100 percent committed to *one* change. It will take an all-out effort. And it will probably be the hardest thing you've ever done! But that one change has the potential to make a 100 percent difference in your life.

One Risk

One sentence.

> *After Ehud came Shamgar son of Anath, who struck down six hundred Philistines with an oxgoad.*

That's the only attention Shamgar gets in Scripture. But look again — this *one* line tells me everything I need to know about him. One farm tool and one decision end up saving the entire nation of Israel. This one risk was a huge deal.

Israel was in spiritual anarchy and political tyranny. They did some straight-up evil and their punishment was enslavement to the Philistines, who ruled with intimidation and fear. But one man refused to be ruled by that fear. Next to David, Shamgar has to rank as one of history's most improbable heroes. And just like the shepherd-turned-king, this farmer-turned-warrior transformed this makeshift cattle prod into a weapon of war. I don't think Shamgar had a clue while he was driving oxen that God would turn his oxgoad into the instrument of Israel's deliverance.

Shamgar was a one-man army. All he had was an oxgoad, which was basically a long stick. But he knew that if God was for him, no one could stand against him. So Shamgar grabbed his oxgoad and charged the enemy armies. He looked as dumb as David coming at Goliath with a dinky slingshot. But courage doesn't wait until the situation is in your favor. It doesn't wait until a plan is perfectly formed. It's not a war of politics. Courage only waits for one thing: a green light from God.

A Little Crazy

Like Shamgar, Cori Wittman grew up on a farm. And we all know that while you can take a farmer's daughter off the farm, you can't take the farm out of a farmer's daughter. After college, Cori moved to DC and started working on Capitol Hill. She got involved at National Community Church and led one of the most unique small groups in our history as a church. Cori decided to launch a group for women on *agricultural policy*. I honestly didn't think a single soul would show up, but more than a dozen women ended up joining the group! And that was just the beginning.

Cori went on our first mission trip to Thailand to work with The Well. It's a ministry that rescues women out of the sex industry. Cori prayed something quite dangerous on that trip: *Lord, break my heart for the things that break Your heart.* Famous last words! One conversation with a Thai farm girl who ended up in Bangkok's red-light district because of circumstances beyond her control did just that. Cori came back to the United States, but she left her heart in Thailand. She decided to quit her job and move to Thailand as a full-time missionary. She started out working during the night shift in the red-light district of Bangkok, ministering to women trapped in the web of the sex trade. She's now trying to stop the problem before it starts by piloting a program for teens in rural Thailand. This single twenty-something chick from Idaho is mentoring and mothering seven teenage girls!

Cori shared some of her doubts and dreams in a blog post titled "A Little Crazy Goes a Long Way."

> Can I really be an adequate interim parent for teenagers abandoned by their mom until God provides more permanent foster parents? Will God heal a faithful and faith-filled couple that just discovered they are HIV positive and protect their unborn baby from the disease? Will my friend reach his goal of staying clean from meth for an entire year and grow as a committed husband and father? Will God build a movement to create real change in rural communities to stop this cycle of family and community brokenness that so often leads to participation in the sex industry?

I love Cori's answer to her own questions:

> I'm beginning to realize a little crazy goes a long way when you're talking kingdom crazy. Some of my questions won't be answered for months or years, but I am standing on God's promise that He is able to do immeasurably more than all we can ask or imagine. Sometimes my faith falters, and feelings of inadequacy, loneliness, and smallness cloud my vision. And I get overwhelmed at the task at hand. But when I put my faith glasses on, all things are possible.

She wasn't looking for excuses! If she was, everything above would've been easy to talk herself out of. Cori was looking for opportunities, and this one was disguised as an impossible problem. Most people run away from their problems, but Shamgars run at them with their oxgoads.

Thailand is a non-confrontational culture, which means people just don't talk about problems, and so change is challenging. But Cori is *gracefully* challenging a problem head-on. She's also helping harvest this year's rice crop with her adopted teenage daughters.

That's what going all out for Christ is all about. I'm not saying right now you need to dump school and move, but there are practical ways of attacking problems you notice in your school or job or even a youth group. It's all about attacking problems with whatever oxgoad God has given you. It's an assault on darkness by being salt and light. You can't point out problems and hope they fix themselves. Let yourself to be part of the solution, the hands and feet of Christ.

Here Am I

As you may have learned from Moses, God doesn't call the qualified; He qualifies the called! So hopefully that'll help you open your mind to God's call and foster availability and teachability in you. If you're willing to go when God gives you a green light, He'll take you to some great places to do impossible things. That's how a farmer's daughter ended up in rural Thailand. She was *willing*. And sometimes it's as simple as that.

> Then I heard the voice of the Lord saying, "Whom shall I send? And who will go for us?"
> And I said, "Here am I. Send me!"

Abraham. Jacob. Joseph. Moses. Samuel. David. Isaiah.

They all have one thing in common. Every one of them said, "Here am I."

All we have to do is simply say, "Here am I" and God will take it from there! Don't stress about money or your age or parents. It'll happen in time! It's God's job to get us where He wants us to go, not ours. Our job is to be available anytime, anyplace. Sometimes it's a simple prompting to go out of our way to love our next-door neighbor or the kid sitting alone at lunch. Sometimes it's a calling to move halfway around the world or sometimes it's moving over one lunch table. But it always starts with the little three-word prayer: *Here am I.*

That's what Samuel said when he heard the still small voice of the Holy Spirit.

That's what Moses said at the burning bush.

That's what Caleb said when he finally stepped foot into the Promised Land.

That's what Isaiah said when King Uzziah died.

And that's what Cori said after her trip to Thailand.

You need to be willing to do something a little crazy!

Shamgar may have been the least qualified person to deliver Israel. For starters, he likely wasn't even an Israelite. It would've been so easy to talk his way out of it: *I don't have the right weapon. I can't do this by myself. These aren't even my people.* If we look for an excuse, we'll always find one! If we don't, we won't. When it comes to making excuses, we are infinitely creative. What if we channeled that creativity into finding *solutions?*

Redefining Success

You never know what relationship, skill, experience, or attribute God will use in you! He used a beauty pageant to strategically make Esther queen of Persia and stop the genocide of the Jews. He used Nehemiah's cupbearer-skills to position him for a royal favor that would end up rebuilding the wall of Jerusalem. He used David's musical chops to open the palace door and give him access to the king of Israel. He used Joseph's imprisonment and his ability to interpret dreams to save two nations from a famine. And He used the intensity of a mass-murderer named Saul to spread the gospel, while writing half of the New Testament in the process.

If God used *them*, He can use you. There are some real block-heads in the Bible, but fortunately, if you're reading this, you must be pretty smart! And so you're clever enough to know He wants to use you. He's cultivating talents within you right now that will serve His kingdom in ways that you had no idea were possible. It could be athletic abilities or musical skills that God uses to give you a platform. It may be your creative genius. It may be something you don't even like about yourself! No matter what it is, just make sure He gets the praise for your excellence (which He gave you)!

Do the best you can with what you have where you are.

That's my definition of success. It's not based whether or not you get rich, powerful, or famous. And it's not based on past experience or future potential. It's maximizing every opportunity in every way, every second of time, every ounce of talent, and every penny of money.

It doesn't matter whether you end up a journalist, teacher, entrepreneur, artist, politician, or lawyer. What matters is that you use your oxgoad for God's purposes. Don't just make a living — make a difference! You really don't need to change friends, churches, or schools to do that. You might, but first and foremost, you need to change *you*.

Enough Is Enough

Shamgar knew that if he was going to go down, he was going to go down fighting. And that's the key to deliverance, whether it's from the Philistines or pride or prejudice or pornography.

You've got to go on the offensive! Pick a fight!

There comes a point when *enough is enough*. We know we can't continue down a path we're on because it's a dead end. Relationally, physically, or spiritually. It may not kill us, but it will eat us alive! So you have to decide that enough is enough — you've had enough of whatever it is that's eating you alive!

You've got to grab your oxgoad and go for it.

Take the mission trip or set up the counseling appointment. Whatever it has to be.

The Plains of Hesitation

George W. Cecil once said, "On the Plains of Hesitation bleach the bones of countless millions who, at the Dawn of Victory, sat down to wait, and waiting — died!" Basically a bunch of soldiers hesitated to go into battle and sat around waiting ... and died waiting!

I'm both a procrastinator and a perfectionist. That magical combination means I have to discipline myself to make decisions and set *deadlines*. I've learned that indecision *is* a decision. But let me tell you: one of the keys to getting anything done is simply setting deadlines. Dreams without deadlines aren't going to happen.

When it comes to going after goals, the first step is always the longest and the hardest. We have a tendency to keep doing what we've always done. Unless we commit to a new course of action, we'll maintain our current rhythms and routines. It's also known as the *status quo bias*.

In 1965, a study was done on the campus of Yale University. Graduating seniors were educated about the dangers of tetanus and given the opportunity to get a free vaccination at the health center. While a majority of the students were convinced they needed to get the shot, only 3 percent followed through and got the vaccine.

Another group of students was given the same lecture but was also given a copy of the campus map with the location of the health center circled on it. They were then asked to look at their weekly schedules and figure out when they would find the time to get the shot. More than nine times as many students got vaccinated.

Good intentions aren't good enough! It only makes sense that you're more likely to go through with something if you have a written *plan*. You need to make the call or make the move. Don't get stuck on the Plains of Hesitation.

The Enemy often tries to discourage us by overwhelming us. We need to counter this by breaking down our goals into smaller steps. I don't know if you can overcome anorexia for the rest of your life, but I believe you can win the battle *today.* And the same goes for any challenge you face.

Don't worry about next week or next year. Can you resist temptation for twenty-four hours? Can you win the battle for one day? I know you can. And so does the Enemy.

Take it one day at a time!

One Step at a Time

A few years ago, I climbed Half Dome at Yosemite National Park. I remember looking up at the summit and thinking, *How am I going to make it to the top?* The answer was really quite simple: *one step at a time.* If we keep putting one foot in front of the other, it's amazing how far we can go!

The hardest part of the hike wasn't physical. It was mental. The last leg was a sixty-degree slope to the summit that looked like a ninety-degree climb to someone who is afraid of heights. I'm afraid of heights. When I finally got to the top of Half Dome, I sat down on a large rock and noticed that someone had etched something into the rock: *If you can do this, you can do anything.*

Something inside of me clicked because I knew it was true. I decided to attempt something I hadn't been able to do in five years of trying. I was packing 225 pounds, which isn't terribly overweight on my six foot three inch frame, but I knew I'd feel better and live longer if I could tip the scales at sub – 200. I made a defining decision to do it, and then I made a daily decision to exercise more and eat less. In two months I dropped twenty-five pounds. I also dropped my cholesterol by fifty points. And I felt five years younger.

We spend far too much energy focusing on the very thing we

cannot control — the outcome. What if I fall back into my bad habit? What if I don't hit my target weight or don't get my dream job?

Don't worry about results. If it's the right thing, the results are God's responsibility. Focus on doing the right thing for the right reason. And don't buy into the lie that it can't be done! It will take all-out effort, but you can do all things through Christ, who gives you strength.

A failed attempt is not failing.

Failing is not trying.

If you are trying, you are succeeding.

That's what going all out is all about.

It's giving it everything you've got.

So grab your oxgoad and go for it.

ALL
IN ALL

CHAPTER 12

SDG

Johann Sebastian Bach was a master musician, to say the least. He has 256 cantatas to his name. I personally dig *Jesu, Joy of Man's Desiring*. It's epic. Four-hundred-something years after its original writing, it's still one of the most popular sound tracks to the bridal entrance at a wedding ceremony.

Bach's music is about more than melodies and harmonies. It's the motivation behind the music that makes it so beautiful and outstanding and unique. The reason *Toccata and Fugue in D Minor* or *Mass in B Minor* touch the soul is because they *come* from the soul. Bach's cantatas didn't originate as music. They were prayers before they were songs, literally. Before Bach started scoring a sheet of music, he would write a little *J.J.* — *Jesu, juva* — at the very top. It's a pretty simple prayer: *Jesus, help me*.

Then, when he would finish a composition, Bach wrote three letters in the margin of his music: SDG. Those three letters stood for the Latin phrase, *Soli Deo Gloria* — *to the glory of God alone*. His life was a unique translation of that singular intention to give only God glory. So is yours. No one can glorify God *like you* or *for you*. Your life is an original score!

Imagine if filmmakers and entrepreneurs followed suit. What kind of cultural impact would we have if our scripts and business plans originated as prayers? Imagine students scribbling SDG on their essays for AP American History, or doctors scrawling SDG on their prescriptions. It'd be a little weird but sort of cool.

It's not about *what* you do. It's about *why* you do what you do. And ultimately, it's about *who* you do it for.

In God's kingdom, our motivations matter the most. If you do the "right" thing for the wrong reason, you're doing the wrong thing. Sorry prudes of the world, but if you're staying out of trouble because you think you're cooler or better than anyone else, you're wrong. God judges the motives of the heart, and He only rewards those who do the right thing for the right reason. To be perfectly honest, I think I've forfeited a fat chunk of my reward because I do things for myself.

SDG is living for the One person in the audience who matters. It's doing the right thing for the right reason. You only need one person's approval — the applause of nail-scarred hands.

Just Jesus.

Nothing less, nothing else.

And God Sang

To Johann Sebastian Bach, there was no difference between "spiritual" and "secular." All things were created *by* God and *for* God. Every note of music. Every color on the palette. Every flavor of Skittles.

Arnold Summerfield, the German physicist and pianist, noticed that a single hydrogen atom, which lets off one hundred frequencies, is more musical than a grand piano, which only lets off eighty-eight frequencies.

Every single atom is a unique expression of God's creative genius. And God can create better music with an atom you can't see than with a giant grand piano. Every atom is a unique expression of worship. That's cool.

Composer Leonard Bernstein believed that the best translation of Genesis 1:3 isn't "and God said." He believed a more accurate translation would have been "and God sang." The Almighty sang every atom into existence, and every atom echoes that original melody sung in three-part harmony by the Father, Son, and Holy Spirit.

Whale songs can travel thousands of miles underwater. Meadowlarks have a range of three hundred notes. Stars emit sounds too!

Research in "bioacoustics" has revealed that we're surrounded by millions of ultrasonic songs. Supersensitive sound instruments have discovered that even earthworms make faint sounds! Lewis Thomas put it this way: "If we had better hearing, and could discern the descants [singing] of sea birds, the rhythmic tympani [drumming] of schools of mollusks, or even the distant harmonics of midges [flies] hanging over meadows in the sun, the combined sound might lift us off our feet."

The songs we can hear audibly are only one instrument in the symphony orchestra that is creation. Someday, heavenly eardrums will reveal millions of songs we could never hear with the human ear.

Then I heard every creature in heaven and on earth and under the earth and on the sea, and all that is in them, saying:

"To him who sits on the throne and to the Lamb
be praise and honor and glory and power,
for ever and ever!"

In the meantime, we'll settle for Bach.

The Chief End of Man

The first little line of the Westminster Shorter Catechism (maybe you've heard of it) is worth memorizing.

Man's chief end is to glorify God, and to enjoy Him forever.

I don't think it can be said any simpler or any better. We exist for one reason and one reason alone: *to glorify God, and to enjoy*

Him forever. It's not about you at all. It's all about Him. But you do get to enjoy Him! And that's worth the while.

Soli Deo Gloria makes life make sense. It's not about success and failure. It's not about good days and bad days. It's not about wealth or poverty. It's not about health or sickness. It's not even really about life or death. It's about glorifying God in whatever circumstance you find yourself in.

Whenever. Wherever. Whatever.

There is no circumstance where you can't find a way to glorify God. That's why living SDG is so sweet! It's a way of life.

Whatever

As a parent of two teenagers, *whatever* isn't exactly my favorite word! It's so dismissive and jerky, but I think it's redeemable. It's one of my one-word prayers to God now. *Whatever* can be a statement of straight-up surrender.

Remember Gethsemane? The garden where Jesus literally wrestled with the will of God? When He said, "Take this cup from Me," He was talking about the cup of wrath. Jesus knew He'd have to drink that whole thing, but before He did, He asked the Father if He would take it away and if there was *any* other way. But then He made sure to frame his request within a prayer: "Not My will, but Yours be done."

This was *Jesus'* all in moment. Yes even *Jesus* had an all-in moment. He was 100 percent human! This was His *whatever* prayer.

There are two great little *whatever* verses in Scripture. Both start with the same all-inclusive phrase: *whatever you do.*

Whatever you do, work at it with all your heart, as working for the Lord, not for human masters.

The phrase *with all your heart* means "with more energy than you have." It means giving it everything you've got — 100 percent.

And then some. The issue isn't *what* you're doing. The real issue is *why* you do it, *how* you do it, and *who* you do it *for*. That's key!

Ultimately, I hope when you get a full-time job you'll love what you do and do what you love. I hope you work at a job that you would want to do even if you didn't get paid to do it. But sometimes you need to have a job you don't like, and you need to still glorify God by doing a good job at a bad job. At least you have a job!

One of my summer jobs during college was working as a ditch digger. Yes, a *ditch* digger. We called ourselves earth relocation engineers, but it was backbreaking work that was impossible for anyone on earth to enjoy. But I made the most of it. Anybody can do a good job at a good job, but there is something God-glorifying about doing a good job at a bad job. Anybody can be nice to a nice boss or teacher, but there is something God-glorifying when you love like Jesus in a godless work or school environment.

Mundane Miracles

Now here's the other *whatever* verse.

> So whether you eat or drink or whatever you do, do it all for the glory of God.

How do you even eat and drink for the glory of God? Sometimes the Bible says some strange stuff.

Paul is using the daily rituals of eating and drinking to make a point: *even the most mundane activities can be absolutely miraculous*. Mundane, as in your routine, your day-in and day-out activities like eating and drinking. You take close to 23,000 breaths every day. When was the last time you thanked God for *one* of them? The process of inhaling oxygen and exhaling carbon dioxide is a fairly complicated respiratory task, as I'm sure you know from biology, that requires physiological precision. We tend to thank God for the things that take our breath away. And that's fine. But maybe we should thank Him for the breath itself, seeing as it's a miracle!

Give and Take Away

No one in the history of mankind has lost more in less time than Job. He lost everything... His family, his health, and his wealth: gone in a matter of moments. It's hard enough *reading* the book of Job; imagine *living* through it. He endured unbelievable heartache and unimaginable loss. But when his world falls apart, Job falls to the ground in worship.

> *Naked I came from my mother's womb,*
> *and naked I will depart.*
> *The LORD gave and the LORD has taken away;*
> *may the name of the LORD be praised.*

A few years ago, Jason and Shelly Yost started an organization called New Rhythm. It advocates for adoption. Their lives are devoted to helping orphans find families and helping families find orphans.

Not long ago, Jason and Shelly chose to adopt. After going through the lengthy legal process, they adopted a little girl they named Mariah. But a few days after taking her into their home, she was taken out of their hands by the birth mother, who changed her mind during the ten-day revocation period. It was awful for Jason and Shelly.

I saw them a few days later at a retreat where I was speaking and Jason was leading worship. The first song he sang was "Blessed Be Your Name." The lyrics are inspired by the story of Job. In fact, the chorus restates this very verse: *You give and take away*. When Jason started singing the chorus, I about *lost it*. I knew how hard it was for him to sing those words. But I also knew how much he meant them.

I have some Bible verses that are fallback verses for me. I fall back on the things I *know* to be true. This is one of those verses. I don't want to minimize any loss you've gone through in your life, but I do want to remind you there is nothing you possess that wasn't given to you by God. It's His nature to give and give and give. But we're subject to the world, which can take away. But there is *one* thing that can never be taken from you, and that is Jesus Christ. And if you have Jesus, then you have everything you will ever need for all of eternity! It's a very simple equation.

Everything – Jesus = Nothing
Jesus + Nothing = Everything
Just like that.

CHAPTER 13

THROW DOWN YOUR STAFF

Then the LORD asked him, "What is that in your hand?"
    "A shepherd's staff," Moses replied.
    "Throw it down on the ground," the LORD told him.
So Moses threw down the staff, and it turned into a
snake!

Exodus 4:2–3 NLT

Nearly a hundred years ago, the Philadelphia Church in Stockholm, Sweden, sent two missionary couples to the Congo. David and Svea Flood, along with Joel and Bertha Erickson, macheted their way through the jungle to establish a mission. The first year was pretty rough and they didn't have a single convert. The village was pretty resistant to the gospel because they were afraid of offending their tribal gods, but still Svea loved them and shared Jesus with a five-year-old boy who delivered fresh eggs to their back door every day.

Svea became pregnant not long after arriving, but she had malaria during most of the pregnancy. She gave birth to a baby girl, Aina, in 1923, but Svea died seventeen days later. David made a casket and buried his twenty-seven-year-old wife on the mountainside overlooking the village. Imagine the grief and bitterness. David gave his daughter, Aina, to the Ericksons and returned to Sweden with dashed dreams and a broken heart. He'd spend the next five decades as a drunk.

The Ericksons raised Aina until she was a toddler, but both of them died within three days of each other (the villagers actually poisoned them to death). Aina was given to an American missionary couple, Arthur and Anna Berg. The Bergs renamed their adopted daughter Agnes, and called her Aggie. They eventually returned to America to pastor a church in South Dakota.

After high school, Aggie enrolled at North Central Bible College in Minneapolis, Minnesota. She met and married a fellow student, Dewey Hurst. They started a family of their own and served a number of churches as pastors. Then Dr. Hurst became president of Northwest Bible College. On their twenty-fifth wedding anniversary, the college gave the Hursts a special gift — a trip to Sweden. Aggie's sole purpose was to find her biological father who had abandoned her fifty years before. They searched Stockholm for five days without a trace. Then, on the last day before departure, they got a tip that led to the third floor of a rundown apartment building. There they found Aggie's dad, who was on his deathbed with a failing liver.

The last words David Flood ever expected to hear were, "Papa, it's Aina." And the first words out of his mouth were filled with remorse: "I never meant to give you away." When they embraced, fifty years of bitterness melted away. A father and daughter were reconciled that day, and a father reconciled with his heavenly Father for eternity. When Aggie landed in Seattle the next day, she received news that her father had passed away while they were in flight.

Now here's the rest of the story.

Five years later, Dewey and Aggie Hurst attended the World Pentecostal Conference in London, England. Ten thousand delegates from around the world gathered at Royal Prince Albert Hall. One of the speakers on opening night was Ruhigita Ndagora, the superintendent of the Pentecostal Church in Zaire. What caught Aggie's attention was the fact that Ruhigita was from the region where her parents had been missionaries half a century before. After the message, Aggie spoke to him through an interpreter. She asked if he knew of the village where she was born, and Ruhigita told her he had grown up in that village. She asked if he knew of missionaries by the name of Flood. He said, "Every day I would go to Svea Flood's back door with a basket of eggs, and she would tell me about Jesus. I don't know if she had a single convert in all of Africa besides me." Then he added, "Shortly after I accepted Christ, Svea died and her husband left. She had a baby girl named Aina, and I've always wondered what happened to her."

When Aggie revealed that she was Aina, Ruhigita Ndagora started to sob. They embraced like siblings separated at birth. Then Ruhigita said, "Just a few months ago, I placed flowers on your mother's grave. On behalf of the hundreds of churches and hundreds of thousands of believers in Zaire, thank you for letting your mother die so that so many of us could live."

Sometimes going all in feels like it's all for nothing.

But it's not over until God says it's over! God's greatest victory so far was won on the heels of what seemed like His defeat on Calvary. Three days after His *crucifixion*, Jesus walked out of His tomb under His own power.

You won't win every spiritual battle, but the war has already been won two thousand years ago. It was the deathblow to death itself! And we're basically conquerors because of what Christ did.

If you go all in for the cause of Christ, there'll definitely be some setbacks. But remember this: without a crucifixion there is no resurrection! And when you have a setback, you don't take a step back, because God's setting up your comeback.

David and Svea Flood didn't have a single convert they *knew* of. They thought it was a waste. But one seed obviously took root and blossomed beyond what they could've believed.

You've probably heard of the ripple effect — this was a big one. All because of one act of obedience.

It will never be all for nothing. I promise you that. So does Scripture!

The Patron Saint of Second Chances

For forty years, Moses felt like he had failed to accomplish his God-ordained dream of delivering the Israelites out of slavery. The prince of Egypt had all the potential in the world at forty, but he felt like a lost cause at eighty. Moses lost everything when he lost his temper. He became both a felon and a fugitive because of it. Instead of doing God's will God's way, he took matters into his own hands and ended up killing an Egyptian taskmaster. And by trying to expedite God's will, he delayed it for four decades!

You might feel passed by at some point in your life. Your dream seems like a lost cause. Reality just doesn't measure up. But the "crisis" presents us with a choice: throw in the towel once and for all or throw our hat back in the ring. Too many people give up. They call it quits because they feel like it's too late. But Moses is the patron saint of second chances. And third. And tenth. And hundredth. No matter how many wrong turns we've taken and no matter how many detours we've been down, it's God's grace that gets us back into the party.

Moses was left to rot with a bunch of sheep in the desert for forty years. But it had a purpose. God had already given Moses forty years of the easiest class on the list: *Palace 101*. Now Moses had to pass *Wilderness 101*.

The irony of the Exodus story is that even though Moses thought he was unqualified, God used every past experience to prepare him for his date with destiny. No one knew the palace like the *prince* of *Egypt*. After all, he grew up in the thing! And after tending sheep for forty years, he knew the ways of the wilderness — the wildlife, the watering holes, the weather patterns. The sheep were practice for the Israelites, who were basically sheep! It's like David killing bears and lions; it probably helped when he had to floor a giant.

Going all in for God isn't something you do once. You'll probably get it wrong more than once before you get it right. But it's just as important as success. Failure is the fertilizer that grows character — which means success won't backfire on you.

Triumphal Procession

Paul writes some good words in his letter to the Corinthians:

> *But thanks be to God, who always leads us as captives in Christ's triumphal procession and uses us to spread the aroma of the knowledge of him everywhere.*

The promise in 2 Corinthians 2:14 hints at a Roman tradition. After winning a great victory, the Roman army marched through the streets of Rome with all their captives. The "triumphal procession" started at the Campus Martius and led through the streets to the Circus Maximus, around Palatine Hill, and on to Capitoline Hill.

I've stood under the triumphal arch that's the Via Triumphalis (the road they went down during the procession). It's downright epic. More than five hundred of these triumphal processions passed under it during the reign of the Roman Empire.

Our triumphal procession begins at the cross of Christ. Jesus is our Conquering King, and we're the captives in His train, set free from sin and death. Surrender *is* the first step of faith. Then going all in is following in the footsteps of Jesus wherever they may lead us.

Every triumphal procession has a point of origin. And that certainly includes Israel's exodus out of Egypt. If you backtrack all the way to the beginning, the journey to the Promised Land starts at a burning bush.

The Element of Surprise

Moses lived on the backside of the desert staring at the backside of sheep for four decades. In case you care, that's over twenty-one million minutes. His life was defined by monotony until he had an epiphany. Then, on a day that started out like the 14,600 days before, Moses heard a voice calling his name from a burning bush.

I really like this moment because the burning bush reveals the playful side of God's personality. You best expect the unexpected because God is predictably unpredictable! But this one takes the cake, doesn't it? A talking bush is about as crazy as a talking donkey ... Oh, wait, He did that too!

Jesus definitely got the mischief gene from his Father. When He was twelve, Jesus "missed" the caravan back to Nazareth and was hanging out with the rabbis at the temple. I bet some of those same rabbis were on duty twenty years later when Jesus turned the temple upside down by single-handedly throwing out the money changers. Can you say *surprise*? Jesus walked on water, turned water into wine, and healed a shriveled hand on the Sabbath. Those are classy miracles, but they're also sarcastic and playful! He's always messing with the Pharisees.

Back to the burning bush. Why did God reveal Himself that way?

I wonder if it's for the same reason that the angels announced the birth of the Messiah to night-shift shepherds instead of religious scholars. I wonder if it's for the same reason that the Messiah was born to a peasant couple who came from the wrong side of the tracks instead of a priestly family in the holy city.

God loves the element of surprise!

Holy Ground

Jewish scholars used to debate why God revealed Himself to Moses in the middle of nowhere. Why the burning bush on the backside of the desert? Why not a highly populated or religiously significant place? Why would God go so far out of His way? The consensus was that God wanted to show "that no place on earth, not even a thornbush, is devoid of the Presence."

God is everywhere to be found.

God is where you want to be.

God is where *it's at.*

The theological word is *immanence.*

And it's the complement to *transcendence.*

He is God Most High.

He is also God Most Nigh.

God is above, but He's not just "up there." He's beneath, but He hasn't fallen and "can't get up." He's outside, but He's not on the outs. He's inside, but He's not confined or restricted. God is above all things presiding, beneath all things sustaining, outside of all things embracing and inside of all things filling.

As I said earlier in this book, sometimes I end a service at NCC with this phrase (it captures this concept pretty well): *When you leave this place, you don't leave the presence of God. You take the presence of God with you wherever you go.*

You're standing on holy ground all the time.

But remember that holy ground is not the Promised Land.

It's right here, right now. It's wherever God is, and God is everywhere! Every moment is a holy moment.

When you go all in with God, you never know how or when or where He might show up. But God can invade the reality of your life at any given moment and change everything for eternity. And when He does, you need to mark that spot or moment somehow. Like building an altar! Make a creative altar to The Lord.

I have a picture of a cow pasture in Alexandria, Minnesota, hanging behind my desk. That cow pasture is essentially my burning bush. It's where I felt called to ministry at the age of nineteen.

The chapel balcony at Central Bible College is holy ground. Every day during my senior year of college I paced and prayed on it like nobody's business. That's where I learned to hear the still, small voice of the Holy Spirit.

National Community Church owns an $8 million piece of Promised Land on Capitol Hill where we'll build a future campus. It took a failed contract and a financial miracle to land that piece of Promised Land. The spiritual breakthrough happened late one night with my son and a good friend. We hit our knees and claimed it for God's glory one night. And boom! It's ours. When we break ground, we'll creatively mark that spot as holy ground.

And finally, Pennsylvania Avenue is my Via Triumphalis. On the heels of our failed church plant in Chicago, Lora and I visited my college roommate, who had moved to DC. I felt called to the nation's capital as we were driving down Pennsylvania Avenue somewhere between the Capitol and White House.

Who Am I?

When God revealed His plan to Moses, Moses wasn't too keen on it. He had a pretty impressive list of excuses, starting with his stuttering problem. He summarized his insecurities by simply saying, "Who am I?" But that's the wrong question. It's not about *who* you are. It's about *whose* you are! And I love God's answer: "I AM WHO I AM." God answers his questions by revealing His name. And He also offers this encouragement: "I will be with you."

That's all we need to know, isn't it? If God is for us, who can be against us?

His name is the answer to every question. His name calms every fear, seals every prayer, and wins every battle.

Angels bow and demons quake at His name. That's so awesome!

Who you are is absolutely irrelevant. God doesn't use us *because* of us. He uses us even though we usually screw up His plan. It's not like heaven is going to go broke if *you* don't tithe. The Creator doesn't *need* you. And even if you take your talents elsewhere, it's not like the kingdom of God is losing an all-star player. But regardless, God has chosen to accomplish His plans through ordinary people. We just have to throw down our staff to get in the game.

Let Go and Let God

Then the LORD asked him, "What is that in your hand?"
"A shepherd's staff," Moses replied.
"Throw it down on the ground," the LORD told him. So Moses threw down the staff, and it turned into a snake!

Exodus 4:2 – 3 NLT

Throwing down your staff is letting go and letting God. As in letting God do His thing. This section is for all of the control freaks of the world (me included)! One of our pastors, Joel Schmidgall, likes to say, "You can have faith or you can have control, but you can't have both." If you want God to do something cool, you have to take your hands off the controls.

You have to loosen your grip on *your* staff. The staff represented Moses' identity and security as a shepherd. It was the way Moses made a living. It was also the way he protected himself and his flock. So when God told Moses to throw it down, He was essentially asking Moses to let go of who he was. It was like God asking you to throw down your car, girlfriend or boyfriend, your iPhone, whatever! Whatever defines you and whatever you find your security in.

It was Moses' all in moment.

What are you holding on to? Or maybe I should ask, what are you not willing to let go of? If you aren't willing to let go, then it's pretty obvious that you're not in control of that thing, that thing controls *you*. And if you don't throw it down, your staff will forever remain a staff. Lame. It will always be what it currently is. Still lame. But if you have the courage to throw down your staff ... well, you probably know how the story goes.

All in All

On June 7, 1857, a Scotsman named Thomas Maclellan made a covenant with God, whom he called his *All in All*. This is what it read:

> *O God of Heaven, record it in the book of Thy remembrances that from henceforth I am Thine forever. I renounce all former lords that have had dominion over me and consecrate all that I am and all that I have, the faculties of my mind, the members of my body, my worldly possessions, my time, and my influence over others, all to be used entirely for Thy glory.*

That covenant, made on his twentieth birthday, was renewed on his fiftieth and seventieth birthdays. More than five generations later, the seed he sowed is still multiplying in the millions of dollars that are given away by his family.

So basically, in English, he just gave up all his wants and desires and decided to be a channel for God's blessing. The legacy that Thomas Maclellan left wasn't just wealth, it's a spiritual legacy as well! He threw down his staff. And God blessed his business affairs, because He knew that Thomas Maclellan wouldn't hold on to the blessing. And his family has followed in his footsteps! That's some legacy, right there.

What you hold in your hand can't multiply until you put it into the hands of God. But if you let go and let God, He will use it beyond your wildest imagination. I know that kind of money seems pretty huge if you're making minimum wage. But even if you're generous in much smaller ways, it always comes back around.

What's in Your Hand?

What is that in your hand?

That is the question the Lord asked of Moses.

It's the same question He asks of us.

You may be tempted to say, *Just a staff.* You may be tempted to think: I can't make much of a difference. But if you put the fish and loaves *you* have into God's hands, God can feed five thousand with it.

To us, 5 + 2 equals 7. In God's economy, it equals 5,000, with a remainder of 12. The disciples didn't think two fish and five loaves could make much of a difference, but they obviously underestimated the original Iron Chef. When dinner was done, there were twelve basketfuls left over. There was more left over than they originally started with. What?! That's crazy.

If the little boy had held on to the two fish and five loaves, they would have remained what they were. But in the hands of Jesus, those two fish and five loaves turned into the miraculous feeding of the multitude!

I have a pastor-friend, Chip Furr, who felt called to start a coffee roasting company. It wasn't easy getting it off the ground, but Chip knew he was standing on holy ground. Then one day he got a God-idea—why not recycle the burlap bags that the coffee beans come in? He contacted a company that employs people with disabilities and arranged for them to do the stitching for some fashionable messenger bags and tote bags. He calls it restoration fashion.

What's in your hand? You can hang onto it and it can stay something insignificant. Or hand it over and it can be something epic, like a crocodile-eating snake.

Sir Moses

Moses Montefiore was the first Jew to hold high office in the city of London. A close friend of the royal family, he was knighted Sir Moses by Queen Victoria in 1837—the same year he was elected sheriff of London.

He eventually became famous for his generosity. He made seven trips to the Holy Land (the last one when he was ninety-one). He built a textile factory, a printing press, a windmill, and several agricultural colonies in Palestine.

On Moses's one-hundredth birthday, *The London Times* filled its editorial section with articles all about Sir Moses. In one of them, a conversation was recorded for readers. Someone once asked Sir Moses to reveal his net worth. He had amassed a fortune through business and real estate, and he thought for a moment. Then he named a figure that wasn't quite as big as the questioner thought. He said, "But surely the sum total of your wealth must be much more than that." With a smile, Sir Moses replied, "You didn't ask me how much I own. You asked me how much I am worth. So I calculated how much I have given to charity this year. We are worth only what we are willing to share with others."

What's *your* net worth? And it has nothing to do with the trophies in your case or the awards on your wall.

Your net worth equals the sum total of all you've given away. Time *and* money.

Not a penny more.

Not a penny less.

And when everything is said and done, what you don't share is lost forever. But what you put into the hands of God becomes an eternal keepsake.

Throw down your staff.

CHAPTER 14

TAKE
A STAND

"King Nebuchadnezzar, we do not need to defend
ourselves before you in this matter. If we are thrown
into the blazing furnace, the God we serve is able
to deliver us from it, and he will deliver us from Your
Majesty's hand. *But even if he does not, we want you to
know, Your Majesty, that we will not serve your gods or
worship the image of gold you have set up.*"

Daniel 3:16–18; italics added

In 1888, Alfred Nobel got to read his own obituary. Whoops.
A French newspaper mistakenly printed it after the death of
his brother Ludvig. They referred to the Swedish inventor as
"the merchant of death" and said that he made it possible to
kill more people more quickly than anyone in history. Awkward . . . That sent a little shock through Alfred's soul. It actually
became a defining moment for him that would change his life
and legacy.

Alfred Nobel was granted 355 patents during his lifetime, but
his most famous was for nitroglycerine mixed with absorbent
sand, which was shaped into sticks called dynamite. His invention
made digging tunnels and building dams and canals a million

times easier. It saved time, money, and a lot of lives. But like any invention when you put in the wrong hands, dynamite became a nasty weapon. So Alfred Nobel devoted the rest of his life, and his death, to redeeming that invention.

Nobel rewrote his last will and testament after reading his obituary. On November 27, 1895, he pushed all of his chips to the middle of the table and decided to use his $9 million fortune to establish one of the most coveted awards in the world — the Nobel Prize. A hundred years later his name reminds you of the world's greatest advancements in science, literature, medicine, and peace. The good resulting from that award is way more than the harm dynamite's done.

That's Alfred Nobel's legacy.

Few things are as life-changing as a near-death experience. I've experienced it myself! Believe me, ruptured intestines are no fun! My twenty-nine-year-old brother-in-law, Matt, had open-heart surgery followed by emergency surgery two weeks later. Talk about near death. He'd tell you death is a mirror that gives us a glimpse of who we really are. It's a *rearview* mirror that puts the past into perspective.

Every day should be lived like the first day and last day of your life! After all, it is. It has never been before, and it will never be again. You've got to make every day count.

I celebrate two birthdays every year. One is my biological birthday, November 5. The other is the day I should have died, July 23. And to be honest, the second is more meaningful than the first.

I'm living on borrowed time. The truth is, all of us are!

Near-death experiences are often defining moments in our lives. And I don't know of a near-death experience that's more intense than Shadrach, Meshach, and Abednego being chucked into a furnace.

Death Sentence

It was a death sentence.

Shadrach, Meshach, and Abednego knew that if they didn't bow down to the statue of King Nebuchadnezzar, their goose was cooked. But they obviously feared God more than they feared death. They would've rather died in that furnace (supposedly the most painful possible death) than *dishonor* God. So they made a defining decision to stand up for what was right rather than bow down to ninety feet of wrong-ness. All or nothing, now or never, life or death.

To be honest, I could've come up with a million reasons to bow down to that sucker. *I'm bowing on the outside, but I'm not bowing on the inside. I'll ask for forgiveness right after I get back up. My fingers are crossed. I'm only breaking one of the Ten Commandments. What good am I to God if I'm dead?* When it comes to sinful rationalizations, we get very creative. But it's our lame rationalizations that block His revelations.

When we lose our integrity, we don't leave room for divine intervention. When we take matters into our own hands, we take God out of the picture. When we try to manipulate a situation, we miss out on the *miracle.*

Stop and think about this.

If Shadrach, Meshach, and Abednego had just bowed down to the statue, they would have been delivered from the fiery furnace. But it would have been by Nebuchadnezzar, not by God. And it would have been *from*, not *through*. They would have lost the epic testimony by failing the test.

Their integrity triggered the miracle.

Their integrity made it possible for God to show up (show off really).

Their integrity became their fire insurance and life insurance.

Epic Integrity

To bow or not to bow?

That's the real question.

Your boss or best friend probably hasn't constructed a ninety-foot-tall statue of himself or herself recently. But I wouldn't be surprised if they told you to cut a corner here or hook up with someone there. Don't bow down. Lose your job or friend before you lose your integrity! Yes, of course I'm dead serious!

It was integrity that got Shadrach, Meshach, and Abednego in trouble with Nebuchadnezzar, but it was that same integrity that found them favor with God. So which is it? To bow or not to bow? Because you can't have it both ways! I'd rather get in a little trouble with King Nebuchadnezzar than get in trouble with God. And I'd much rather find favor with the King of Kings than with King Nebuchadnezzar.

We put our reputation at risk with stuff like this. But when we obey God, we come under the umbrella of His protective authority. He's our Advocate and Supporter. And it's His reputation that is at stake. If we don't give the Enemy a foothold, God won't let him touch a hair on our head.

Not a hair on their heads was singed, and their clothing was not scorched. They didn't even smell of smoke!

That's pretty ridiculous. Integrity will keep you out of the fiery furnace, but it can just as well keep us from getting *burned*. It protects and affects those around you! When you exercise integrity in tempting situations, God can often make a dramatic entrance, just like He did with Shadrach, Meshach, and Abednego. Three men were thrown into the furnace, but a fourth man was ready and waiting to reward their righteousness. And He's still waiting. The Redeemer wants to rescue us, but by faith we have to put ourselves in that dangerous position.

Protective Instincts

Once upon a time, our family vacationed at a friend's cabin in Deep Creek, Maryland. It was in a pretty densely wooded area where we wouldn't have been surprised to bump into Bigfoot. There weren't really any Sasquatch sightings, unfortunately, but we were warned that hungry brown bears would show up every now and then looking for leftovers. Late one night, I decided to get into the hot tub (it was fancy by cabin standards) with Parker and Summer. It was cold and snowy, so steam was rising. The trees formed a canopy that blocked the moonlight, so it was pitch black. And all we could hear were the sounds of the deep woods … Truth be told, the kids were downright scared. And so was I! Your imagination plays games when you can't see a thing.

In an overly dramatic voice, I made a fatherly declaration to my children: "If a bear came out of these woods and attacked us, I want you to know that I would die for you." Our kids were six and eight at the time. Let's just say that my words were far from reassuring. They ran into the house screaming, and it's a miracle they aren't scarred to this day!

I maybe could've delivered that a little differently, but I'll never forget what I felt. I meant what I said! I would die for my children without a moment's hesitation under any circumstances!

That right there is the heavenly Father's deepest impulse toward us. Anyone who messes with you messes with Him. His protective instincts are pretty obvious at the cross. That's where the Creator stepped between every sinner (that's you and I) and Satan. That's where the *Advocate* took on the *Accuser* of the brethren. The Sinless Son of God took the fall for us!

The cross is God's way of saying, "You're totally a hundred percent worth dying for."

When that life-giving truth penetrates into the deepest place in your heart, it transforms how you think, feel, and live. Perfect love casts out all fear. You become fearless even when you are defenseless. But turn the coin over and ask yourself this: *Is He worth dying for?*

Going all in and all out for the All in All is both a death sentence and a life sentence. Your sinful nature, along with its selfish desires, is nailed to the cross. Then, and only then, does your true personality, your true potential, and your true purpose come alive. After all, God cannot resurrect what has not died. And that's why so many people are half alive. They haven't died to self yet.

Don't Play Defense

Who are you going to offend?

That is one of the most important decisions you'll ever make!

If you fear man, you'll offend God.

If you fear God, you'll offend man.

It's a bit of a tough predicament, I know. But Jesus certainly wasn't afraid of offending Pharisees. In fact, He turned it into an art form. I totally live by the motto: *thou shalt offend Pharisees!* Or in this case, thou shalt offend Nebuchadnezzar!

Shadrach, Meshach, and Abednego didn't want to offend the king. Nebuchadnezzar *gave* them their reasonably powerful jobs so they owed him a lot. So not bowing down to his statue was like biting the hand that feeds you, but the only other option was biting the hand of God ... Not happening!

So. Who're we going to offend?

This will be good advice for when all of you get famous. I've discovered that the more influence someone has, the larger the target on his or her back becomes. People take potshots at you. I've had a decent amount as an author and a pastor. Here's my approach.

Don't play defense. Life's just too short to spend all of my time and energy defending myself. God is my Judge and Jury. Abraham Lincoln lived by this phrase (I try to too): "You can please all of the people some of the time, and some of the people all of the time, but you can't please all of the people all of the time." It's particularly difficult when the person's name is Nebuchadnezzar. But no matter how you slice it, the fear of God is the beginning of wisdom, and the fear of man is the beginning of foolishness.

My friend and mentor Dick Foth once told me about a deal he struck with God: *If I don't take the credit, then I don't have to take the blame*. I like that! A lot!

Look in Proverbs:

It is to one's glory to overlook an offense.

That's one of the most-circled promises in my Bible. I want to be impossible to offend because of God's grace. If God has forgiven me for every offense, how can I take offense at someone else's sin? God sure doesn't. If I take offense, I get defensive, and I stop playing offense with my life. That's right where Satan wants you.

Jesus didn't even defend Himself before Pilate — when His life depended on it. He didn't defend Himself when the soldiers whipped His back, spit in His face, and put a crown of thorns on His head. He sure didn't when they killed Him! Is it really such a pain to forget about remarks made behind your back by some insecure kid?

Jesus had a legion of angels that were one phone call away, but He didn't dial. He didn't defend Himself, and He didn't take offense. Better yet, He gave them one of these: "Father, forgive them, for they do not know what they are doing."

Ninety-Foot-Tall Ego

Shadrach, Meshach, and Abednego didn't defend themselves. They just let the tides take their course and acted according to their beliefs and let the chips fall where they may. That's what going all in is all about. It's refusing to bow down to what's wrong. And even more, it's standing up for what's right. When Nebuchadnezzar saw this whole thing unfold, he changed his ways. Unfortunately, he took it too far *again*, and threatened to tear the limbs off anyone who didn't bow down to the God of Shadrach, Meshach, and Abednego.

Can you say *controlling*?

I think it's safe to say that anyone who builds a ninety-foot-tall statue of themselves is probably a little insecure somewhere. That statue is the definition of pride. Nebuchadnezzar definitely ranks high on the list of history's egomaniacs. But we all have a little Nebuchadnezzar in us, don't we? We'd never build a ninety-foot-tall statue, but we get upset when people don't bow down to our *desires*. That's true. We'd never throw someone into a fiery furnace, but our anger heats up when we don't get our way.

If you don't find your identity and security in what Christ did for you on the cross, you will try to hide your insecurities behind your hypocrisies.

You'll just try to fight your own battles.

You'll try to create your own opportunities.

You'll try to establish your own reputation.

And you'll quickly discover that manipulating is *exhausting*.

Just ask Saul ... Scripture says he kept a jealous eye on David — he was more concerned about his reputation than God's reputation.

Two verses point to two defining moments in his downfall.

Then Saul built an altar to the LORD; it was the first of the altars he built to the LORD.

And then one chapter later:

Saul went to the town of Carmel to set up a monument to himself.

Somewhere between 1 Samuel 14:35 and 1 Samuel 15:12, Saul stopped building altars to God and started building monuments to *himself*. And the prophet Samuel saw right through the smoke screen: "Although you may think little of yourself, are you not the leader of the tribes of Israel?"

You know who builds monuments to themselves? Insecure people! Pride is a by-product of insecurity. And the more insecure a person is, the more monuments they need to build.

There is a fine line between *Thy kingdom come* and *my kingdom come*. If you cross the line, your relationship with God becomes self-serving. Then it's not even a friendship or any kind of relationship, it's just you being a parasite. You aren't serving God, you're using Him. You aren't building altars to God. You're building monuments to yourself.

And there's a name for that: idolatry.

Take a Stand

The word *integrity* comes from the root word *integer*. Hopefully we all passed Algebra 1 and know that this refers to a whole number and not a fraction. In other words, integrity is *all in*. It's whole. Not partial. Integrity is an all-or-nothing kind of thing.

Is there anything you're bowing to? Be honest here. Then it's time for us to take a stand!

And it always starts with the little things.

That's the last thing you wanted to hear, right? You won't go all the way, but maybe just second or third base? Sorry, but that little compromise can cost you your future potential. Trust me, I've experienced the same temptations. I was a teenager once too. If you give the enemy an inch, he'll take a mile. Don't touch sin with a ten-foot pole. Are you going to have guts like Joseph, or lose your spine on something so insignificant?

It's all about epic integrity.

And that's something to be celebrated. We live in a culture that celebrates talent more than integrity, but we've got it backward. Talent fades over time. If you're good at basketball, you'll only get worse as you get older! Believe me. So do intellect and appearance. It all fades. You'll eventually lose your strength and lose your looks. Heck, you might even lose your mind. But you don't have to lose your integrity. Integrity is one of the only things that doesn't lose value over time. Nothing takes longer to build than a godly reputation. But you can lose it all on one sin streak — that's why it should be celebrated and protected.

Your integrity is your legacy.

Your integrity is your destiny.

Take a stand.

CHAPTER 15

THIRTY PIECES OF SILVER

Then Judas Iscariot, one of the twelve disciples, went to the leading priests and asked, "How much will you pay me to betray Jesus to you?"
And they gave him thirty pieces of silver.

Matthew 26:14–15 NLT

A guy named Walter Mischel (a psychologist at Stanford University) did a series of tests in 1972 that would become known as the *marshmallow test*. The original study was done at Bing Nursery School with kids between four and six. He offered one marshmallow to each child, but if the child could resist eating it right away, he or she was promised two marshmallows instead of one. Sounds like a deal, right? The researchers analyzed how long children could resist the temptation. Some kids grabbed the marshmallow the second the researchers walked out of the room. Others mustered as much willpower as they could, employing a variety of temptation-resisting tactics. They sang songs, played games, covered their eyes, or talked to themselves the entire time. A few of them even tried to go to sleep. The test was all about *delayed gratification*.

The point was to see what effect delayed gratification had on eventual academic achievement. Walter tracked the academic record of the 216 children who participated all the way through high school graduation. When those results were paired up with the delayed gratification times, researchers found a dramatic difference between the "one marshmallow now" and "two marshmallows later" kids. The kids who were able to delay gratification longer were way more academically accomplished. They scored, on average, 210 points higher on the SAT. Big difference!

The two-marshmallows-later kids were also more social. There was a noticeable difference in self-reliance and self-confidence. In a follow-up study done when these children were in their early forties, researchers found that the two-marshmallows-later children had higher incomes, stronger marriages, and happier careers.

Cutting to the chase: delay of gratification is a powerful indicator of future success in any endeavor.

The biblical word for this is *exousia*. And the best English translation may be *supernatural self-control*. It's not something we can really do ourselves. It's one of the nine fruits of the Spirit! And I don't think it's an accident that it's the last one listed. It takes the longest and might be the toughest to master.

The New Testament makes a distinction between two types of power:

Dunamis is the power to do things beyond our natural ability.

Exousia is the willpower to *not* do things we have the ability to do.

Whether we're pursuing a goal or breaking a bad habit, we need *exousia*. Our long-term success depends on our ability to delay gratification. It's true with you and your boyfriend or girlfriend, with your job, school work, and certainly your relationship with the Lord. It's what going all in is all about. Instead of living for the here and now, it's living for the day when we stand at the pearly gates!

I like what C. T. Studd said: "Only one life, 'twill soon be past; only what's done for Christ will last."

One marshmallow now?

Or two marshmallows later?

Thirty Pieces of Silver

If the marshmallow experiment had been done with the twelve apostles, Judas Iscariot would have been a "one marshmallow now" kind of guy. He couldn't keep his hand out of the cookie jar. He betrayed Jesus (*the Son of God ...*) for thirty pieces of silver. His lack of integrity from the get-go says a lot.

He was a thief, and having charge of the moneybag he used to help himself to what was put into it.

Judas' famous betrayal wasn't a spur-of-the-moment mistake. He betrayed Jesus each and every time he took a little something— something for himself from the money pot. And while most of us can't imagine pickpocketing Jesus, we do it all the time in a thousand different ways. We rob God of the glory He demands and deserves by not living up to our full, God-given potential.

No matter how we slice it, sin leaves us with the short end of the stick. Sin always over-promises and under-delivers. Righteousness pays for eternity. Yet we sell out for one marshmallow now instead of holding out for two marshmallows later.

Esau sold his birthright for a bowl of stew.

Samson sold his secret for a one-night stand.

Judas sold his soul for thirty pieces of silver.

What were they thinking? You're right, they weren't. Nothing is more illogical than sin. It's just poor judgment. And we have no alibi, except the cross of Jesus, who is Christ.

It's not worth it, and we know it.

Yet we do it anyway.

We sell out for something dead *lame*, instead of going all in for something so excellent.

C. S. Lewis described this tendency to sell God short very well:

> It would seem that Our Lord finds our desires, not too strong, but too weak. We are half-hearted creatures, fooling about with drink and sex and ambition when infinite joy is offered us, like an ignorant child who wants to go on making mud pies in a slum because he cannot imagine what is meant by the offer of a holiday at the sea. We are far too easily pleased.

Thirty pieces of silver. That was Judas's price point. Jewish readers would have recognized that amount as the exact amount to be paid if a slave was accidentally killed under Mosaic law. Judas sold his soul for the replacement value of a slave.

The silver coins were most likely sanctuary shekels, since he was paid off by the chief priests. And while some estimates range higher, each coin may have been worth as little as seventy-two cents! So in today's currency, Judas betrayed Jesus for $21.60.

A Little Judas

We don't know a ton about Judas from Scripture, but theories are plenty. Some scholars suggest Judas was a weak-willed coward with a manipulative wife pulling the strings. Others believe Judas betrayed Jesus out of pure greed (even though $21.60 isn't much). And some suggest he had revolutionary aspirations. He wanted a political savior, and when Jesus didn't meet his expectations, he flew the coop.

And we do the same thing, don't we? When God doesn't conform to our expectations, we're tempted to betray what we believe in. Like Judas, the mind wanders because a lot of the time we're in it for what we can get out of it. So when God doesn't grant our wishes like a genie in a bottle, we're tempted to turn our back on Him.

This is what separates the adults from those over at the kiddie table. How do you react when God doesn't meet your expectations? If you've just invited Jesus to follow you, you probably throw a fit when you don't get your way. If you're truly following Jesus, and not just a fair-weather friend, you won't bail on Him when the weather gets bad or the road gets bumpy.

As I've said before, it's difficult to analyze someone's thought process who lived thousands of years ago, but it's safe to say Judas was spiritually schizophrenic. Aren't we all? Our love is mixed with lies. We steal from the One we have supposedly surrendered our lives to. And we betray Him in our own unique ways.

There is a little Judas in all of us. And any of us are capable of betraying God if we allow the fear of people to outweigh the fear of God, selfish ambition to strong-arm godly ambition, or sinful desires to short-circuit God-ordained passions.

Long Shadows

The betrayal of Judas was foretold by the prophet Zechariah five hundred years before it happened. But that doesn't mean it was set in stone. God has given us free will. So for better or for worse, the choice is ours.

History turns on a dime.

The dime is our defining decisions.

And those decisions, right or wrong, determine our destiny.

Some defining decisions are obvious, like choosing a career, a college or a spouse eventually. But most are made in the shadows, like Judas did. Of course, they eventually come into the light. And it's those defining decisions that cast the longest shadows.

I think of Joseph resisting Potiphar's wife. He had no idea how that one choice would alter his life and the course of history. And doing the right thing didn't pay any dividends for seventeen years. In fact, it seemed to backfire when Joseph landed in jail. But our decisions, right or wrong, always catch up with us sooner or later. That two-marshmallows-later decision would save two nations from being destroyed by a famine two decades later.

I think of David making a split-second decision not to kill King Saul when he had him cornered near the Crags of the Wild Goats. He could have claimed self-defense. And no one would have seen him do it. Except God ...

Of course, David made his fair share of one-marshmallow-now decisions too. He did a little window peeping from the palace porch. And after sleeping with Bathsheba, he tried to cover it up by having her husband Uriah killed. That's not cool.

Bad decisions usually lead to worse decisions. After Judas betrayed Jesus, he made the worst and last decision of his life. He hung himself from a tree in a potter's field. It's a sad ending and a standing warning.

The good news is that God can forgive our bad decisions. And one good decision can totally change the course of our lives. And that one good decision will lead to better decisions. But it starts by making the right decision when no one is looking.

What defining decision do you need to make?

What risk do you need to take?

What sacrifice do you need to make?

And So Life Is

An Irish author by the name of George William Russell wrote a dark piece of poetry in 1931 titled "Germinal."

> *In ancient shadows and twilights*
> *Where childhood had strayed*
> *The world's great sorrows were born*
> *And its heroes were made.*

In the lost boyhood of Judas
Christ was betrayed.

Judas didn't decide to betray Christ after following Him for three years. The seeds of betrayal were planted in the soil of his youth. Our most important choices, good and bad, have the longest genealogies. Take it from me being farther along in age: seize your youth. One bad decision can't ruin you, but when you're trying to make the right decisions, you're headed in the right direction.

The Austrian psychotherapist Alfred Adler was famous for beginning counseling sessions with his catchphrase: "What is your earliest memory?" No matter how the patient answered, Adler responded, "And so life is." Adler believed that our earliest memories shape us, psychologically. And in my experience, that is most definitely true.

One big piece of my personality traces back to an incident that happened when I was four years old. It might also reveal a little Judas in me. A five-year-old friend who lived four doors down had a bike that I would "borrow" quite often. Sometimes I got permission. Sometimes I did not. So one day he proudly informed me that I could no longer ride his bike because his father had removed the training wheels. I took it as a challenge. I marched down to his house, hopped on his bike, and made my maiden voyage without training wheels. To top it off, I parked *his* bike in *my* driveway.

If you want me to do something, don't tell me to do it. Tell me it can't be done, and I will try to do it. That's just the way I'm wired. And so life is.

We know next to nothing about Judas as a toddler, teenager, or beyond. But I'm guessing he threw temper tantrums when he didn't get what he wanted because that infantile self-centeredness is still evident when the woman with the alabaster jar anoints Jesus. Judas has to make a fuss.

"That perfume was worth a year's wages. It should have been sold and the money given to the poor."

Judas should have been up for an Oscar with that performance. He could not have cared less for the poor. He wanted to be a pawn star — that perfume would've made him a pretty penny. A lot more than $21.60!

It is much easier to *act* like a Christian than it is to *react* like one. That right there is the truth! And Judas's reaction in this situation is pretty revealing. He wasn't all in — he was in it for what he could get out of it.

Are we any different?

The Talmud says that there are four kinds of people in the world.

The first person says, *What's yours is mine.*

The second person says, *What's yours is yours.*

The third person says, *What's mine is mine.*

And the fourth person says, *What's mine is yours.*

Which one are you?

The first person is obviously jealous and greedy. That's Judas. That's one end of the spectrum. The second and third persons *seem* neutral, but Jewish rabbis believed it to be a fundamental misunderstanding of the created order. Nothing belongs to us, not even us. Only the fourth person is righteous, because they have discovered that the secret to joyful living is sacrificial giving! And we aren't really giving anything up. We're simply returning what God loaned to us in the first place.

The Second Sin

Original sin is the sin Adam and Eve committed when they bought the Enemy's lie that God was holding out on them. They ate from the tree of the knowledge of good and evil because they did not believe that God was all in. If you believe that God is holding out on you, you won't go all in with God. So the second sin recorded in Scripture (the first outside Eden) is a stepchild of the original sin. Cain held back — just like his parents.

Abel was all in. He brought God the best of the best — his choice lambs.

But Cain held out. He gave God leftovers — the throwaway part of his harvest.

Nothing has changed. The choice is still ours to make — hold out on God or go all in.

Isn't that the lesson to be learned from Ananias and Sapphira? They gave the proceeds from a property sale to the church, but God struck them dead. What!? Why? Because they bald-faced lied about being all in. They claimed they had given up every-thing, but they kept a little pocket change.

The true value of an offering isn't measured by how much we give. It's measured by how much we *keep*. Look at the widow. She gave two copper coins — less than anybody else, but she kept nothing for herself. That's why Jesus honored the little boy who gave five loaves and two fish. It wasn't much, but it was everything he had.

By definition, a sacrifice must involve sacrifice. Cain gave what he didn't even really want or couldn't use. There was no sacrifice in the sacrifice. He kept the best and gave the worst. And that's never been good enough for the All in All.

Gold, Frankincense, and Myrrh

The story of the Magi is dumbed-down a lot for well-intentioned Christmas sermons once a year, but the Wise Men deserve a lit-tle more attention. They stand directly opposite to Judas. Judas sold out for some silver coins. The Magi bought in with gifts of gold.

At first, it seems like the Magi bring the wrong gifts to this baby shower, doesn't it? What kid wants a bottle of frankincense, right? Get the poor kid an ancient Jewish action figure — David with live-action slingshot or something.

It reminds me of a thing I came across on the Internet titled "The Three Wise Women."

> *Do you know what would have happened if it had been three wise women instead of three wise men? They would have asked for directions, arrived on time, helped deliver the baby, cleaned the stable, made a casserole, and brought practical gifts.*

Gold, frankincense, and myrrh seem like misguided gifts, but stop and think about it. How does a minimum-wage carpenter who just paid a huge tax bill fund a trip to a foreign country? These gifts were just what Mary and Joseph needed. They were their golden ticket to Egypt! And it's the only way they could have escaped the genocide. Those gifts saved their lives. The Magi's gifts were Mary and Joseph's miracle!

And the same is true for us. Giving is one way we get in on God's miracles. Your gifts of gold, frankincense, and myrrh will translate into someone else's miracle.

Maybe it's time to quit looking for the easy way out and go the extra mile. Quit expecting Jesus to follow you and make the decision to follow Him.

Think Long

In 1976, Apple, Inc., was cofounded by three men. Steve Jobs, who eventually became the chairman and CEO, is the most famous of the three. You've probably even heard of Steve Wozniak, the mastermind who invented the Apple I and Apple II computers. But you probably haven't heard of the third member of the Apple trinity, Ronald Wayne. It's Wayne who sketched the first logo, created the first manual, and wrote the original partnership agreement.

You probably don't give a hoot about stocks, but there's a point to this. Ronald Wayne was a 10 percent shareholder in Apple. There are now 940 million active shares worth about $500 per share. So that 10 percent stake would be worth at least $47 billion today. But less than two weeks after getting his 10 percent share, Ronald Wayne sold out for $800.

Don't be Ronald Wayne!

More importantly, don't be Judas Iscariot!

Judas lost more than Wayne ... the Kingdom of God.

When everything is said and done, our biggest regret will be whatever we didn't give back to God. It'll be lost for eternity. But the time, talent, and treasure we invest in His kingdom will earn compound interest for eternity.

A lot of people will spend their whole lives accumulating the wrong things. Start divesting yourself of those things that will depreciate over time and start investing in those things that will appreciate throughout all eternity.

Stop selling out to sin.

Stop selling God short.

For the millionth time: It's time to go all in.

ALL OR NOTHING

CHAPTER 16

THE IDOL THAT PROVOKES TO JEALOUSY

> The Spirit lifted me up between earth and heaven and in visions of God he took me to Jerusalem, to the entrance of the north gate of the inner court, where the idol that provokes to jealousy stood.
>
> Ezekiel 8:3

God is not jealous *of* anything. He can't be. But the Creator is jealous *for* everything because it all belongs to Him. Including you and me.

"There is not a square inch in the whole domain of our human existence over which Christ, who is Sovereign over all, does not cry, 'Mine!'" Abraham Kuyper said that. That's good stuff right there.

Everything was created by Him ... for Him.

There never has been and never will be anyone like you, but that's thanks to the God who created you. And that means no one can worship God *like you* or *for you*. You're downright irreplaceable in God's grand scheme. And God is jealous for you.

He's the one who causes your synapses to fire. He's the one who conceives desires within your heart of hearts. He's the Dream Giver. He's The Word. That's pretty cool to be so intensely sought after by someone so excellent.

That's why all in and all out is the base line.

That's why He will settle for nothing less than all in and all out.

Double Jealousy

If you've been around church long enough, you know God has many, many names. It may seem like a human invention, trying to be creative. But each one says something different and important about God. There are more than four hundred names for God in the Bible, and each one reveals a dimension of who He is. One of those names is revealed to Moses on Mount Sinai:

> "Do not worship any other god, for the LORD, whose name is Jealous, is a jealous God."

Catch the double emphasis?

Have you ever seen the T-shirt tagline, The Department of Redundancy Department? I, for one, find that funny! I don't even know why, but it's probably the same reason I find this verse fascinating. God isn't just jealous. He's doubly jealous. And when God says something more than once, it might be a bright idea to think twice about what it means.

You don't belong to God once. You belong to God twice!

Once because He created you.

Twice because He redeemed you.

He gave us life through creation. And when we were dead in our sin, He gave us eternal life through redemption. We don't owe Him one life. We owe Him two lives! And that is why God is doubly jealous.

Jealousy isn't a character trait that we sing about or write about often. We ignore it because we don't understand it. Jealousy has a negative connotation because for us it's usually the by-product of pride. But God's jealousy is a beautiful expression of God's love. It's a jealous love that wants all of you — all to Himself. And if you've ever been in love, you know what I'm talking about.

Seven Billion to God < Three to Me

I don't think I understood this dimension of love until I became a husband and a father. I'm jealous for my wife. And that's the way it should be. She belongs to me, and I belong to her. I vowed all of me to all of her. It was *for better for worse, for richer for poorer, in sickness and in health*. It's tough to understand, but you'll get it if and when you get married.

A few weeks after our wedding, Lora took a dress to the cleaners, and it was damaged in the dry-cleaning process. When Lora nicely pointed out the problem, the woman called her a liar. I immediately thought of some things to call that woman! Part of what ticked me off is that my wife is the most honest person I know. It wasn't the piece of clothing I cared about, it was the accusation against my wife's *character*. Honestly, I felt a rush of rage. Let's just say it's as close as I've ever come to having the cops called on me. I caused a scene. I was ready to quit seminary and stake out in front of the cleaners. Shut that place down! I look back on that incident with a little bit of embarrassment. I'm sure I overreacted, but it was the jealous love of a newlywed husband. And hey, that love has only grown stronger over twenty years of marriage.

I want my kids to love God first and foremost. But I want them to love mom and pops too! No thought is more painful to me as a parent than the thought of my kids not loving me the way I love them. But they probably can't appreciate the way their mom and I love them until they have their own kids.

If you said to me that two out of my three kids would love me, I would not be satisfied with just two thirds. I would be devastated! I don't love my kids equally. I love them uniquely. And that's how God loves us. His love for you is not just unconditional. His love for you is absolutely *unique*. That's a beautiful thing.

For God so loved the world that He gave His only begotten Son.

I'm sure you know John 3:16, but maybe you've never personalized it. God's love can feel grandiose yet a little impersonal. We know He loves everyone, but because there are billions of people on the planet, and we feel a little lost in the mix. If you're one of many siblings, you know what I'm talking about. You can get lost in the shuffle. More children can spread your parents' attention *more*. But God loves every single child like they're His only one. You can probably understand how devastated I'd feel if one of my kids didn't love me, but have you ever stopped to consider the simple fact that seven billion to an infinite God is a lot less than three is to me!

Just as your love for God is unique, so is His love for you. God's love is not divided seven billion ways. He loves all of you with all of Himself. You are the apple of His eye. There is no question about that because Scripture declares it. The only question that remains is this:

Is He your pearl of great price?

Sex God

The prophet Ezekiel has a vision of an idol that is dubbed "the idol that provokes to jealousy." Scholars believe the idol referenced is the Canaanite goddess of fertility.

So basically their sex god.

We look down on those ancient pagans carving their own idols and then bowing down to some wood statue. Usually an audible scoff follows. But are we any different? Any better? We're just *sophisticated* sinners now.

I don't want to pick on Sin City, but have you ever been to Las Vegas? The god of lust is worshiped openly and freely. But the fact that pornography is a one-hundred-billion dollar industry is proof that the god of lust is also worshiped secretly and addictively everywhere else. What I'm getting at is this: we're still bowing down to the Canaanite goddess of fertility. And like every other idol, it has to be dethroned.

What is your idol that makes God jealous?

For some people, it's as obvious as a girlfriend or boyfriend you're having sex with. For others, it's as sneaky as false humility. The idol that makes you jealous is anything that draws your attention, affection or reliance from God. It's anything that consumes more time, more money, or more effort than our pursuit of God.

Idolatry is anything that keeps you from going all in.

Identifying your idols starts with looking at the way you spend your time and money. I can tell you what my priorities are, but if you really want to know what is most important to me, all you have to do is look at my calendar and my checkbook. They don't lie. They reveal what my true priorities are. They will also reveal the idol that provokes jealousy.

Hidden Rooms

Idolatry isn't a problem. It's *the* problem.

Sin is just a symptom. Idolatry is the root cause. You can't just confess the sin, you also have to dethrone the idol. But to discover what it is, we have to dig a little deeper.

The Canaanite goddess of sex was the most visible idol in the temple, but it was just the tip of the iceberg. When Ezekiel peered through a peephole into a hidden room within the temple, he saw crawling things and unclean animals portrayed on the walls in ancient hieroglyphics.

What's etched on the walls of your mind and concealed in the hidden rooms of your heart?

All of us have hidden rooms — the secret sin that no one sees (except the All-Seeing Eye). It's what you do when no one is looking. It's who you are when no one else is present. It's the place where we conceal our most precious idols. And the Enemy wants you to keep your secret sin a secret. That's how he blackmails us.

As a pastor, I've heard a good amount of confessions. When I was younger, I'd get shocked by some of the secret sins that people confessed — people who seemed to be the epitome of holiness. I'm no longer surprised by sin. I'm surprised by the rare person who has the courage to confess their sin. And that's why my opinion of a person who confesses their sin never goes down. It always goes up.

Our church recently filmed a series of short documentaries. Week after week, courageous individuals shared some of their deepest hurts and greatest struggles. With each testimony, our church grew in grace. When a member of our staff shared about his secret addiction to gay pornography, people opened the door to their hidden rooms. Shame rushed out and grace rushed in. In the book of Revelation, we read that Jesus stands at the door and knocks. A relationship begins when we open the front door, but it doesn't end there. He knocks on the closet doors too! Jesus doesn't just want in. He wants all in!

The Inner Court

Just as the Jewish temple had an outer court and inner court, our hearts have an outer court and inner court. It's not enough to invite Jesus into the outer court. You have to let Him into the inner court. He wants to renovate every corner and crevice of your heart, but you have to open the door to your hidden room. Sometimes, He'll gut a whole room and turn it into something brand new!

C. S. Lewis described it in similar terms:

Imagine yourself as a living house. God comes in to rebuild that house. At first, perhaps, you can understand what He is doing. He is getting the drains right and stopping the leaks in the roof and so on ... But presently He starts knocking the house about in a way that hurts abominably and does not seem to make sense. What on earth is He up to? The explanation is that He is building quite a different house from the one you thought of — throwing out a new wing here, putting on an extra floor there, running up towers, making courtyards. You thought you were going to be made into a decent little cottage: but He is building a palace. He intends to come and live in it Himself.

My friends Judd Wilhite and Mike Foster are the founders of POTSC — People of the Second Chance. They're pretty big on grace, and that's why the church Judd pastors, Central Christian Church, is reaching many people who are far from God. I love their mantra plastered on walls all over the building: *It's okay to not be okay.* I get to preach at his church every once in a while, and I hope this doesn't come across the wrong way, but I've never encountered more people who would seem, by all outward appearances, to be in the running for "least likely to attend church." It felt more like I was at a Vegas show or tattoo parlor. It's downright refreshing! They've created a culture of grace where people don't have to pretend that everything is okay. They don't approve of sin, but they don't hide, judge, or ignore it. Grace is loving people for who they are, where they are. It's loving people *before* they change, not just *after* they change. And that grace is the difference between holy and holier-than-thou. Holiness, in its purest form, is irresistible. That's why sinners couldn't be kept away from Jesus. Hypocrisy has the opposite effect. It's as repulsive to the irreligious as the Pharisees' religiosity was to Jesus.

The Gordian Knot

After revealing what was in the hidden rooms, Ezekiel encounters one more idol at the entrance to the north gate of the temple. He saw women mourning Tammuz, the Babylonian fertility god of spring. The key word is *mourning*. As in, the women were weeping. If you want to identify your idols, you need to follow the trail of your tears or fears, your cheers or jeers. And if you do, you'll come face-to-face with the idols in your life.

That's your Tammuz.

What makes you mad or sad or glad—what ruins your day or makes your day? What triggers your strongest emotional reactions?

How you show emotion isn't the issue.

Neither is *when* or *where*.

The real issue is *why*.

Does your heart break for the things that break the heart of God? That's the question.

The estimated number of unique human emotions range as high as four hundred, but no matter how many there are, we're called to love God with every single one of them. That's what it means to love God with all our heart.

The distance between your knees and the ground is only twenty-four inches, but it's the difference between you standing on your own and transformation. It's not enough to invite Jesus into your mind. You have to open the door to your heart. No door can stay locked. Even the door to your hidden room.

Nothing messes with emotions like sin. And if you sin long enough, it feels like a Gordian knot that seems impossible to untangle. But Jesus Christ went to the cross to undo what you've done. You can break the cycle!

I recently had the privilege of baptizing a man named Josh. He grew up as a pastor's kid, but when he left home, he left the church too. Then Josh moved to Washington, DC, to take a dream job, but at that point, his life was a nightmare.

At some point, I remember thinking that if the nine-year-old me ever met the current me, he wouldn't be mad; he would just fall to his knees crying and praying so hard to God for me to get better. Sadly, life trials kept proving more than I could take, so I continued to sink lower and lower over the years. My family relationships, friendships, jobs, health — all of it spiraled into this big black hole that my so-called life had come to.

Eventually, Josh's aunt invited him to NCC. She convinced him by telling him that the church met in a coffeehouse. He agreed to go, figuring he'd at least get his caffeine fix. But he got a lot more than that. Josh is a pretty big guy, a real tough guy. And that makes his testimony even more powerful.

I couldn't stop crying throughout the entire service. I don't remember what the sermon was, to be honest. What hit me like a ton of bricks was a sense of longing being fulfilled. I had worked so hard over the years to be a loner and to take care of myself that I refused to give anything or anyone an inch of me. But that morning, twenty years of ironclad citadel masonry crumbled, seemingly without effort.

I cannot describe the overwhelming fear and joy that was drowning me during that service. I was so afraid it was all coming apart, all the work I had done over the years to protect myself from the hurts and pains. I worked very hard to separate myself from everything to do with God. But the joy, oh the pure joy — that was what was making me cry, the flood of joy. I hadn't let myself feel it for fear of losing it over the years. I felt like life was flowing back into me or that I was feeling the rays of the sun after being bereft of them for a long lifetime.

I do not feel like I have figured out all the answers to the questions I have always had about God, but I've gained a peace in me from giving myself to God. Long story short, September 30, 2010, I came to DC for what I thought was a dream job, but I quickly found out I came to DC to wake up from my twenty-year nightmare into the light, love, joy, and peace of Jesus Christ.

After Josh's testimony, I was able to recapture a little bit of it with a sentence. *Twenty years of ironclad citadel masonry crumbled.* I don't know what you've built around your heart, but God wants to give it an overhaul. It starts by letting Him in. All in.

Isn't it time?

Time to answer the knock on the door of your heart.

Time to open the door and invite Jesus in.

Time to go all in and all out with the All in All.

CHAPTER 17

ONE DECISION AWAY

Few Americans have shaped the conscience of our country like Jonathan Edwards. He was basically a genius (this kid got into Yale University at the age of twelve). He's buried at Princeton University, where he was president until his death in 1758. Edwards was the author of dozens of *fat* books, both theological and inspirational. His biography of David Brainerd has inspired countless missionaries to go all in with God. And it was Jonathan Edwards who sparked America's First Great Awakening with his sermon, "Sinners in the Hands of an Angry God," which you probably read in American Literature 101. But his greatest legacy is definitely his descendants, which include more than three hundred ministers and missionaries, one hundred and twenty university professors, sixty authors, thirty judges, fourteen college presidents, three members of Congress, and one vice president.

That legacy traces back to a defining moment.

It was Jonathan Edwards's all in moment.

On January 12, 1723, twenty year-old Jon made a written dedication of himself to God. He wrote it out in his diary and revisited it often over the years.

I made a solemn dedication of myself to God, and wrote it down; giving up myself, and all that I had to God; to be for the future, in no respect, my own; to act as one that had no right to himself, in any respect. And solemnly vowed, to take God for my whole portion and felicity; looking on nothing else, as any part of my happiness, nor acting as if it were.

Along with his solemn consecration to God, Edwards formulated seventy goals or resolutions that shaped his faith. Edwards revisited them once a week throughout his life.

Nothing's changed.

If you don't hold out on God, God won't hold out on you.

There's nothing God can't do in and through a person who's fully dedicated to Him. We want to do amazing things for God, but that isn't our job. That's God's job. Our job is to let God do *His* job.

So we stand on the same three-thousand-year-old promise the Israelites did:

"Consecrate yourselves, for tomorrow the LORD will do amazing things among you."

God wants to do amazing things.

So what are you waiting for?

It's now or never.

It's all or nothing.

It's time to go all in and all out.

ACKNOWLEDGMENTS

When everything's said and done, I want to be famous in my home. My family means the world to me. So thanks to my wife of twenty years, Lora. And thanks to our three children — Parker, Summer, and Josiah.

I've had the joy of pastoring National Community Church in Washington, DC, for seventeen years, and I wouldn't want to be anyplace else doing anything else with anyone else. I feel equally called to pastor and to write, and NCC has so graciously afforded me the opportunity to do both. So this book is dedicated to the church I love and serve as lead pastor. It was also inspired by a sermon series at our church titled *All In*. It was a benchmark series for many people who made the life-changing decision to go all in with Jesus Christ.

A special thanks to our entire staff and to our executive leadership team — Joel Schmidgall, Heather Zempel, and Christina Borja.

Authors can write a book by themselves, but publishing a book takes a team effort. Thanks to the incredible Z team. A special thanks to John Sloan and Dirk Buursma, my editors; Chriscynethia Floyd, Alicia Mey, and the entire marketing team; and Tracy Danz for believing in this book. Thanks to John Raymond, Chris Fann, and TJ Rathbun for making the *All In* curriculum an amazing resource for churches. Also thanks to Captain Mike, Jay, and the crew who endured bitter cold to shoot it.

Finally, thanks to Esther Fedorkevich and the entire team at the Fedd Agency for tag-teaming with me on this book.

NOTES

Chapter 2: The Inverted Gospel

Page 16: *The world has yet to see*: Quoted in William R. Moody, *The Life of Dwight L. Moody* (New York: Revell, 1900), 134; see Mark Fackler, "The World Has Yet to See …," *Christianity Today* (January 1, 1990), www.ctlibrary.com/ch/1990/issue25/2510.html (accessed February 11, 2013).

Page 17: *Consecrate yourselves*: Joshua 3:5.

Chapter 3: Draw the Line

Page 20: In ad 44, King Herod ordered: James's martyrdom is the only one mentioned in Scripture. See Acts 12:1–2.

Page 20: And so the bloodbath began: See Grant R. Jeffrey, The Signature of God (Frontier Research, 1996), 254–57.

Page 22: God made him who had no sin: 2 Corinthians 5:21.

Page 23: No good thing does God: Psalm 84:11 ESV.

Page 24: the Rich Young Ruler: Luke 18:18–30.

Page 25: What am I still missing? Matthew 19:20 CEB.

Page 26: parable of the bags of gold: Matthew 25:14–30.

Page 26: If you want to be perfect: Matthew 19:21.

Chapter 4: Charge

Page 35: *awarded the Medal of Honor*: Quoted in Thomas A. Desjardin, *Stand Firm, Ye Boys of Maine: The 20th Maine and the Gettysburg Campaign*, 15th anniv. ed. (New York: Oxford University Press, 2009), 148.

Page 35: *I had deep within me*: Quoted in Andy Andrews, *The Butterfly Effect: How Your Life Matters* (Nashville: Nelson, 2010), 20–21.

Page 36: *Their leader had no real knowledge*: Ibid., 20.

Chapter 5: This Is Only a Test

Page 39: *God tested Abraham*: Genesis 22:1.

Page 40: *Long before God laid the foundation*: See Ephesians 1:3–14.

Page 41: *It was God who gave*: Some scholars infer from Ezekiel 28:13 – 17 that Lucifer led the angelic choirs in heaven. While that conclusion cannot be substantiated, it is one possible interpretation.

Page 41: *Fourteen years' worth of work*: Phil Vischer, *Me, Myself, & Bob: A True Story About God, Dreams, and Talking Vegetables* (Nashville: Nelson, 2006), 196.

Page 41: *If God gives you a dream*: Ibid., 234.

Page 43: *I am no longer my own*: *The Book of Offices* (London: Methodist Publishing House, 1936), 57.

Chapter 6: Burn the Ships

Page 49: *tax collector who put his faith in Christ*: Luke 19:1 – 10.

Page 50: *prostitute who anointed Jesus*: Mark 14:1 – 9.

Page 50: *revival that broke out in Ephesus*: Acts 19:17 – 20.

Page 50: *made a $3,739,972.50 statement*: Based on minimum wage in Washington, DC.

Page 50: *Seek me and live*: Amos 5:4 – 6.

Page 52: *From the days of John the Baptist*: Matthew 11:12 NIV (1984 ed.).

Page 55: *Elisha gets extra credit for making*: 2 Kings 2:14; 4:34; 6:6.

Chapter 7: Crash the Party

Page 58: *The party favors were probably phylacteries*: See Matthew 23:5. Phylacteries were boxes containing Scripture verses, worn on forehead and arm.

Page 64: *Wherever this gospel is preached*: Matthew 26:13.

Page 64: *If this man were a prophet*: Luke 7:39.

Page 66: *True spirituality is*: Michael Yaconelli, *Messy Spirituality*, rev. ed. (Grand Rapids: Zondervan, 2007), 46.

Chapter 8: Rim Huggers

Page 71: *Eternity will not be long enough*: A. W. Tozer, The Pursuit of God (Radford, Va.: Wilder, 2008), 30.

Page 72: *We need to study the Word*: 2 Timothy 2:15.

Page 72: *Well done, good and faithful*: Matthew 25:23.

Chapter 9: Climb the Cliff

Page 76: *Come, let's go over*: 1 Samuel 14:1.

Page 77: *But if they say*: 1 Samuel 14:10.

Page 77: *Perhaps the L*ORD *will act*: 1 Samuel 14:6.

Page 78: *So on that day*: 1 Samuel 14:23.

Page 81: *I will build my church*: Matthew 16:18.

Page 82: *A pair of psychologists*: William J. Gehring and Adrian R. Willoughby, "The Medial Frontal Cortex and the Rapid Processing of Monetary Gains and Losses," *Science* 295.5563 (March 22, 2002): 2279–2282.

Page 83: *My conscience is taken captive*: Henry Bettensen and Chris Maunder, eds., *Documents of the Christian Church*, 4th ed. (New York: Oxford University Press, 2011), 214.

Chapter 10: Build the Ark

Page 85: *The internal volume of the ark*: Christian Information Ministries, "Facts on Noah's Ark," www.ldolphin.org/cisflood.html (accessed February 14, 2013).

Page 87: *If it falls your lot*: Clayborne Carson et al., eds., *The Papers of Martin Luther King Jr.: Birth of a New Age, December 1955–December 1956* (Berkeley: University of California Press, 1997), 457.

Page 87: *Noah did everything*: Genesis 6:22.

Page 88: *Noah found favor*: Genesis 6:8.

Page 89: *No good thing does God*: Psalm 84:11 ESV.

Page 92: *I have fought the good fight*: 2 Timothy 4:7 NLT.

Chapter 11: Grab Your Oxgoad

Page 94: *After Ehud came Shamgar*: Judges 3:31.

Page 96: *Cori shared some of her doubts*: You can follow Cori at www.cultivate.com.

Page 97: *Then I heard the voice*: Isaiah 6:8.

Page 100: *On the Plains of Hesitation*: Bob Kelly, *Worth Repeating: More Than 5,000 Classic and Contemporary Quotes* (Grand Rapids: Kregel, 2003). 169.

Chapter 12: SDG

Page 107: *whale songs can travel*: David Rothenberg, *Thousand Mile Song: Whale Music in a Sea of Sound* (New York: Basic Books, 2008), 205.

Page 107: *meadowlarks have a range*: Lewis Thomas, *The Lives of a Cell: Notes of a Biology Watcher* (New York: Penguin, 1975), 23.

Page 107: *If we had better hearing*: Ibid., 26.

Page 107: *Then I heard every creature*: Revelation 5:13.

Page 108: *Not my will*: Luke 22:42.

Page 108: *Whatever you do*: Colossians 3:23.

Page 109: *So whether you eat or drink*: 1 Corinthians 10:31.

Page 110: *Naked I came*: Job 1:21.

Chapter 13: Throw Down Your Staff

Page 112: *David and Svea Flood*: See Aggie Hurst, *Aggie: The Inspiring Story of a Girl without a Country* (Springfield, Mo.: Gospel Publishing House, 1986).

Page 114: *One of the speakers on opening night*: The Congo was called Zaire from 1971 to 1997.

Page 116: *But thanks be to God*: 2 Corinthians 2:14.

Page 116: *After winning a great victory*: A great victory was considered to be a minimum of five thousand enemy troops.

Page 118: *The consensus was that God*: See Hayim Nahman Bialik and Yehoshua Hana Ravnitzky, eds., *The Book of Legends: Sefer Ha-Aggadah* (New York: Schocken, 1992), 63.

Page 118: *God is above*: A. W. Tozer, *The Attributes of God*, vol. 1 (Camp Hill, Pa.: Wing Spread, 1997), 22.

Page 119: *He summarized his insecurities*: Exodus 3:11.

Page 120: *I AM WHO I AM*: Exodus 3:14.

Page 120: *I will be with you*: Exodus 3:12.

Page 120: *Then the LORD asked him*: Exodus 4:2 – 3 NLT.

Page 121: *O God of Heaven*: "Thomas Maclellan's Covenant with God," Generous Giving.org, http://library.generousgiving.org/articles/display .asp?id=16 (accessed February 14, 2013).

Page 122: *But if you put the two fish*: Matthew 14:13 – 21.

Page 122: *I have a pastor-friend*: Check out www.climbsroast.org.

Page 123: *He contacted a company*: Visit www.sackclothashes.com.

Chapter 14: Take a Stand

Page 128: *Not a hair on their heads*: Daniel 3:27 NLT.

Page 131: *You can please all*: For original rendition, see Alexander McClure, *"Abe" Lincoln's Yarns and Stories* (Philadelphia: International Publishing, 1901), 184: "It is true you may fool all of the people some of the time; you can even fool some of the people all of the time; but you can't fool all of the people all of the time."

Page 131: *It is to one's glory*: Proverbs 19:11.

Page 131: *Father, forgive them*: Luke 23:34.

Page 132: *Then Saul built an altar*: 1 Samuel 14:35 NLT.

Page 132: *Saul went to the town*: 1 Samuel 15:12 NLT.

Page 133: *Although you may think little*: 1 Samuel 15:17 NLT.

Chapter 15: Thirty Pieces of Silver

Page 137: *He was a thief*: John 12:6 ESV.

Page 138: *It would seem that Our Lord*: C. S. Lewis, *The Weight of Glory and Other Addresses* (Grand Rapids: Eerdmans, 1965), 2.

Page 138: *Jewish readers would have recognized*: Exodus 21:32.

Page 138: *So in today's currency*: M. R. Vincent, *Word Studies in the New Testament* (New York: Scribner's, 1887), comment on Matthew 26:15 (calculated in today's dollars).

Page 139: *I think of Joseph resisting*: Genesis 39:6 – 10.

Page 140: *I think of David making*: 1 Samuel 24:8 – 13.

Page 140: *In ancient shadows and twilights*: George William Russell, *Vale & Other Poems* (New York: Macmillan, 1931), 28.

Page 142: *That perfume was worth*: John 12:5 NLT.

Page 144: *Do you know what would have happened*: Anne Jasiekiewicz, *A Laugh a Day: Jokes to Keep the Doctor Away* (Bloomington, Ind.: AuthorHouse, 2010), 18.

Chapter 16: The Idol that Provokes to Jealousy

Page 149: *There is not a square inch*: Abraham Kuyper, *Abraham Kuyper: A Centennial Reader*, ed. James D. Bratt (Grand Rapids: Eerdmans, 1998), 488.

Page 150: *Do not worship any other god*: Exodus 34:14.

Page 152: *For God so loved the world*: John 3:16 NKJV.

Page 152: *the idol that provokes*: Ezekiel 8:3.

Page 153: *When Ezekiel peered through a peephole*: Ezekiel 8:10.

Page 155: *Imagine yourself as a living house*: C. S. Lewis, *Mere Christianity*, anniv. ed. (New York: Macmillan, 1981), 173.

Page 156: *He saw women mourning*: Ezekiel 8:14.

Chapter 17: One Decision Away

Page 159: *I made a solemn dedication*: Edward Hickman, ed., *The Works of Jonathan Edwards* (London: William Ball, 1839), 1:56.

Page 160: *Along with his solemn dedication*: While I don't agree with every resolution made by Edwards, I think they set both a standard and an example for us to follow. Don't just adopt these resolutions. Adapt them. Come up with your own covenant.

For reading purposes, I've changed Edwards's wording "Resolved" to the contemporary phrase "I will." The resolutions can be found at apuritansmind.com, "The Christian Walk: Jonathan Edwards' Resolutions," www.apuritansmind.com/the-christian-walk/jonathan-edwards-resolutions/ (accessed February 14, 2013).

1. I will do whatsoever I think to be most to God's glory, and my own good, profit, and pleasure, in the whole of my duration, without any consideration of the time, whether now, or never so many myriads of ages hence. I will do whatever I think to be my duty and most for the good and advantage of mankind in general. I will do this, whatever difficulties I meet with, how many and how great soever.

2. I will be continually endeavoring to find out some new invention and contrivance to promote the aforementioned things.

3. I will, if ever I shall fall and grow dull, so as to neglect to keep any part of these Resolutions, repent of all I can remember, when I come to myself again.

4. I will never do any manner of thing, whether in soul or body, less or more, but what tends to the glory of God; nor be, nor suffer it, if I can avoid it.

5. I will never lose one moment of time; but improve it the most profitable way I possibly can.

6. I will live with all my might, while I do live.

7. I will never do anything, which I should be afraid to do, if it were the last hour of my life.

8. I will act, in all respects, both speaking and doing, as if nobody had been so vile as I, and as if I had committed the same sins, or had the same infirmities or failings as others; and I will let the knowledge of their failings promote nothing but shame in myself, and prove only an occasion of my confessing my own sins and misery to God.

9. I will think much on all occasions of my own dying, and of the common circumstances which attend death.

10. I will, when I feel pain, think of the pains of martyrdom, and of hell.

11. I will, when I think of any theorem in divinity to be solved, immediately do what I can towards solving it, if circumstances don't hinder.

12. I will, if I take delight in it as a gratification of pride, or vanity, or on any such account, immediately throw it by.

13. I will be endeavoring to find out fit objects of charity and liberality.

14. I will never do anything out of revenge.

15. I will never suffer the least motions of anger to irrational beings.

16. I will never speak evil of anyone, so that it shall tend to his dishonor, more or less, upon no account except for some real good.

17. I will live so as I shall wish I had done when I come to die.

18. I will live so at all times, as I think is best in my devout frames, and when I have clearest notions of things of the gospel, and another world.

19. I will never do anything, which I should be afraid to do, if I expected it would not be above an hour, before I should hear the last trump.

20. I will maintain the strictest temperance in eating and drinking.

21. I will never do anything, which if I should see in another, I should count a just occasion to despise him for, or think any way the more meanly of him.

22. I will endeavor to obtain for myself as much happiness in the other world, as I possibly can, with all the power, might, vigor, and vehemence, yea violence, I am capable of, or can bring myself to exert, in any way that can be thought of.

23. I will frequently take some deliberate action, which seems most unlikely to be done, for the glory of God, and trace it back to the original intention, designs, and ends of it; and if I find it not to be for God's glory, repute it as a breach of the 4th Resolution.

24. I will, whenever I do any conspicuously evil action, trace it back, till I come to the original cause; and then, both carefully endeavor to do so no more, and to fight and pray with all my might against the original of it.

25. I will examine carefully, and constantly, what that one thing in me is, which causes me in the least to doubt of the love of God; and direct all my forces against it.

26. I will cast away such things, as I find do abate my assurance.

27. I will never willfully omit anything, except the omission be for the glory of God; and frequently examine my omissions.

28. I will study the Scriptures so steadily, constantly, and frequently, as that I may find, and plainly perceive myself to grow in the knowledge of the same.

29. I will never count that a prayer, nor to let that pass as a prayer, nor that as a petition of a prayer, which is so made, that I cannot hope that God will answer it; nor that as a confession, which I cannot hope God will accept.

30. I will strive to my utmost every week to be brought higher in religion, and to a higher exercise of grace, than I was the week before.

31. I will never say anything at all against anybody, but when it is perfectly agreeable to the highest degree of Christian honor, and of love to mankind, agreeable to the lowest humility, and sense of my own faults and failings, and agreeable to the golden rule; often, when I have said anything against anyone, I will bring it to, and try it strictly by the test of, this Resolution.

32. I will be strictly and firmly faithful to my trust, that that in Proverbs 20:6, "A faithful man who can find?" may not be partly fulfilled in me.

33. I will always do what I can towards making, maintaining, establishing, and preserving peace, when it can be without over-balancing detriment in other respects. December 26, 1722.

34. I will in narrations never speak anything but the pure and simple verity.

35. I will whenever I so much question whether I have done my duty, as that

my quiet and calm is thereby disturbed, set it down, and also how the question was resolved. December 18, 1722.

36. I will never speak evil of any, except I have some particular good call for it. December 19, 1722.

37. I will inquire every night, as I am going to bed, wherein I have been negligent, what sin I have committed, and wherein I have denied myself; also at the end of every week, month, and year. December 22 and 26, 1722.

38. I will never speak anything that is ridiculous, sportive, or matter of laughter on the Lord's Day. Sabbath evening, December 23, 1722.

39. I will never do anything that I so much question the lawfulness of, as that I intend, at the same time, to consider and examine afterwards, whether it be lawful or not; except I as much question the lawfulness of the omission.

40. I will inquire every night, before I go to bed, whether I have acted in the best way I possibly could, with respect to eating and drinking. January 7, 1723.

41. I will ask myself at the end of every day, week, month, and year, wherein I could possibly in any respect have done better. January 11, 1723.

42. I will frequently renew the dedication of myself to God, which was made at my baptism; which I solemnly renewed, when I was received into the communion of the church; and which I have solemnly re-made this twelfth day of January, 1722 – 23.

43. I will never, henceforward, till I die, act as if I were any way my own, but entirely and altogether God's, agreeable to what is to be found in Saturday, January 12, 1723.

44. I will that no other end but religion, shall have any influence at all on any of my actions; and that no action shall be, in the least circumstance, any otherwise than the religious end will carry it. January 12, 1723.

45. I will never allow any pleasure or grief, joy or sorrow, nor any affection at all, nor any degree of affection, nor any circumstance relating to it, but what helps religion. January 12 and 13, 1723.

46. I will never allow the least measure of any fretting uneasiness at my father or mother. I will suffer no effects of it, so much as in the least alteration of speech, or motion of my eye; and be especially careful of it, with respect to any of our family.

47. I will endeavor to my utmost to deny whatever is not most agreeable to a good, and universally sweet and benevolent, quiet, peaceable, contented, easy, compassionate, generous, humble, meek, modest, submissive, obliging, diligent and industrious, charitable, even, patient, moderate, forgiving, sincere temper; and to do at all times what such a temper would lead me to. Examine strictly at the end of every week, whether I have done so. Sabbath morning. May 5, 1723.

48. I will, constantly, with the utmost niceness and diligence, and the strictest scrutiny, be looking into the state of my soul, that I may know whether I have truly an interest in Christ or no; that when I come to die, I may not have any negligence respecting this to repent of. May 26, 1723.

49. I will that this never shall be, if I can help it.

50. I will act so as I think I shall judge would have been best, and most prudent, when I come into the future world. July 5, 1723.

51. I will act so, in every respect, as I think I shall wish I had done, if I should at last be damned. July 8, 1723.

52. I frequently hear persons in old age say how they would live, if they were to live their lives over again: I will live just so as I can think I shall wish I had done, supposing I live to old age. July 8, 1723.

53. I will improve every opportunity, when I am in the best and happiest frame of mind, to cast and venture my soul on the Lord Jesus Christ, to trust and confide in Him, and consecrate myself wholly to Him; that from this I may have assurance of my safety, knowing that I confide in my Redeemer. July 8, 1723.

54. Whenever I hear anything spoken in conversation of any person, if I think it would be praiseworthy in me, I will endeavor to imitate it. July 8, 1723.

55. I will endeavor to my utmost to act as I can think I should do, if I had already seen the happiness of heaven, and hell torments. July 8, 1723.

56. I will never give over, nor in the least to slacken my fight with my corruptions, however unsuccessful I may be.

57. I will, when I fear misfortunes and adversities, examine whether I have done my duty, and resolve to do it, and let it be just as providence orders it. I will as far as I can, be concerned about nothing but my duty and my sin. June 9 and July 13 1723.

58. I will not only refrain from an air of dislike, fretfulness, and anger in conversation, but exhibit an air of love, cheerfulness, and benignity. May 27 and July 13, 1723.

59. I will, when I am most conscious of provocations to ill nature and anger, strive most to feel and act good-naturedly; yea, at such times, to manifest good nature, though I think that in other respects it would be disadvantageous, and so as would be imprudent at other times. May 12, July 2, and July 13.

60. I will, whenever my feelings begin to appear in the least out of order, when I am conscious of the least uneasiness within, or the least irregularity without, I will then subject myself to the strictest examination. July 4 and 13, 1723.

61. I will not give way to that listlessness, which I find unbends and relaxes my mind from being fully and fixedly set on religion, whatever excuse I may have for it — that what my listlessness inclines me to do, is best to be done, etc. May 21 and July 13, 1723.

62. I will never do anything but duty, and then according to Ephesians 6:6 – 8, to do it willingly and cheerfully as unto the Lord, and not to man; "knowing that whatever good thing any man doth, the same shall he receive of the Lord." June 25 and July 13, 1723.

63. On the supposition, that there never was to be but one individual in the world, at any one time, who was properly a complete Christian, in all respects of a right stamp, having Christianity always shining in its true luster, and appearing excellent and lovely, from whatever part and under whatever character viewed: I will act just as I would do, if I strove with all my might to be that one, who should live in my time. January 14 and July 13, 1723.

64. I will, when I find those "groanings" which cannot be uttered (Romans 8:26), of which the Apostle speaks, and those "breakings of soul for the longing it hath," of which the Psalmist speaks (Psalm 119:20), promote them to the utmost of my power, and I will not be weary of earnestly endeavoring to vent my desires, nor of the repetitions of such earnestness. July 23 and August 10, 1723.

65. I will very much exercise myself in this all my life long, viz. with the greatest openness I am capable of, to declare my ways to God, and lay open my soul to Him: all my sins, temptations, difficulties, sorrows, fears, hopes, desires, and every thing, and every circumstance; according to Dr. Manton's 27th Sermon on Psalm 119. July 26 and August 10, 1723.

66. I will endeavor always to keep a benign aspect, and air of acting and speaking in all places, and in all companies, except it should so happen that duty requires otherwise.

67. I will, after afflictions, inquire what I am the better for them, what good I have got by them, and what I might have got by them.

68. I will confess frankly to myself all that which I find in myself, either infirmity or sin; and, if it be what concerns religion, also to confess the whole case to God, and implore needed help. July 23 and August 10, 1723.

69. I will always do that which I shall wish I had done when I see others do it. August 11, 1723.

70. Let there be something of benevolence in all that I speak. August 17, 1723.

Page 160: *Consecrate yourselves*: Joshua 3:5.

The Circle Maker, Student Edition

Dream Big, Pray Hard, Think Long.

Mark Batterson
with Parker Batterson

Prayer can sometimes be a frightening thing: How do you approach the Maker of the world, and what exactly can you pray for? In this student adaptation of *The Circle Maker*, Pastor Mark Batterson uses the true legend of Honi the circle maker, a first-century Jewish sage whose bold prayer saved a generation, to uncover the boldness God asks of us at times, and to unpack what powerful prayer can mean in your life. Drawing inspiration from his own experiences as a circle maker, as well as sharing stories of young people who have experienced God's blessings, Batterson explores how you can approach God in a new way by drawing prayer circles around your dreams, your problems, and, most importantly, God's promises. In the process, you'll discover this simple yet life-changing truth:

God honors bold prayers and bold prayers honor God.

And you're never too young for God to use you for amazing things.